CRUSH!!!

Always and Forever

Hector Martinez

By reading this document, the reader agrees that under no circumstances is the author responsible for any losses, direct or indirect, that are incurred as a result of the use of the information contained within this document, including, but not limited to, errors, omissions, or inaccuracies.

Table of Contents

Chapter 1: One Night in Baltimore

Madison

"You are going to be late if you plan on keeping that hair appointment today!"

Alexa was trying desperately to attract Madison's attention through the two-way microphones and speakers between the gallery and the operating theatre below.

"I hope you realize I had to call in all sorts of favors for Fabian to squeeze you in," she said, teasing her best friend.

"The who's who of Baltimore are all trying to convince him to do their hair for tonight's event! Madison... are you even listening to me?"

Madison Watson finally raised her head from the intricate angioplasty surgery she was performing. She acknowledged Alexa by nodding her head briefly, and waved one of her tiny, gloved hands. She was completing a procedure she'd performed hundreds of times before.

Better known as the top neurosurgeon at Johns Hopkins Hospital, 33-year-old Madison Watson had worked tirelessly to get to where she was. In the medical community, she was not only well respected, but she was the main driving force behind the fundraising event at the Baltimore Museum of Art that was to occur later that evening.

"I'll meet you downstairs in a few minutes, Lexie!" she called out, using her pet nickname for her friend. Madison had no idea where she would be today had it not been for the continued moral support of Alexa James.

Handing the case over to another member of her surgical team, Madison raced out of the theatre removing her gloves, cap, and mask as quickly as possible, and disposing of her surgical gown in the laundry bin as she left the theatre.

All of 5 foot 5 inches tall, she was beginning to break into a jog through the passages of the hospital, all the while untangling her raven-black hair from being confined in one place. Shaking her head as she ran, she finally saw Lexie casually standing, waiting for her with a broad grin on her face, comically tapping the face of her watch. The two entered one of the elevators that would take them directly to the underground parking area.

"So glad you could finally make it!" Lexie said laughing, as she pulled out of the staff parking lot.

"Now to get you ready for this evening. You really know how to cut things fine, girlfriend."

Lexie headed downtown towards *Fabian's*, which was the most exclusive hairstylist in the Baltimore area. Nothing but the best was going to be good enough for her friend, especially after the six months of hell she'd had coming out of a more than toxic marriage to David Webb.

"Let's get that hair of yours looking simply fabulous Maddie darling..." Fabian crooned as he surveyed what Madison's hair currently looked like. "We simply cannot have the belle of the ball looking like this, especially not tonight!"

Fabian had been Madison's stylist of choice whenever she was attending an extra special event. The salon was all abuzz with anyone who could afford their services. The price tag was a steep one, yet well worth it. He could turn even the most drab and dull hair into something magnificent.

By the time he'd finished with her hair, what had previously looked like a bad case of bedhead was now a glamorous up-style with glorious curls cascading halfway down her back. Several fine ringlets of curls framed her perfectly oval face. Madison could hardly believe the complete transformation as she stared at her own reflection in the salon's mirrors.

"Oh Fabian, it looks gorgeous! Thank you for working your magic, as usual."

Alexa and Madison headed toward the Baltimore Museum of Art where they had been given access to a private suite to change their clothes before the evening's event. Madison, still trying to wrap her head around the fact that the masquerade-themed fundraiser in aid of her research work had been sold out, was distracted.

With a capacity crowd of 500 people and hefty price tag of $5,000 per plate, there was no way that Madison could have ever predicted that her brainchild would have raised a cool $2,500,000 even before the auction had begun.

"Lexie, be a dear and help me with this zipper? It's almost 6:30 and I promised the auctioneers I would check in with them by 7:00."

Lexie pulled the zipper up and stared at her friend with her mouth hanging open.

"What? Lexie, do I have something on my face?"

"You look absolutely beautiful. I can't believe that this dress fits you so perfectly! I wish that Dr. Dweeb could see you now!"

The Dr. Dweeb who Lexie was referring to was Dr. David Webb, trauma surgeon at Johns Hopkins and Madison's ex-husband. Only Lexie really knew and understood all the drama that David had put Madison through. David was insufferable and since the divorce, he had realized exactly how much Madison did for him. He was now trying his best to win her back—not that he really wanted her. David needed a nursemaid, or a housemaid. He needed someone to cook for him, and to clean for him.

He was probably the only man that Madison knew who could burn water. There was no way she was ever going to fall for his stories and excuses again. She'd heard all his lies before and all of his promises to change. After four years of marriage and almost as many years of putting up with his lying and cheating, Madison had finally called it quits and filed for divorce.

Six months of legal battles followed. To this day, she had no clue why he was trying to salvage the marriage when it had been in tatters almost from day one. David was a compulsive liar. The only thing he did better than lie, was cheat.

Apart from him being a relatively successful doctor, she really couldn't identify what any woman would see in him. He was quite ordinary to look at. Since their divorce, Madison was able to look at the relationship in hindsight and often found herself wondering what she saw in him in the first place, although there was a brief initial attraction.

Having six months to analyze their relationship from start to finish, helped her see that all they really had in common was their love of medicine. The sex wasn't even that great, which made her understand why none of his conquests had stuck around for long.

Why am I even thinking about David? Tonight is my night! I've worked damn hard for this and not even thoughts of asshole David are going to spoil it for me. The goal is to fund the research division.

She turned to look at herself in the floor-to-ceiling mirror.

Okay, that's why Lexie had her mouth hanging wide open like she was a Venus flytrap... Could that reflexion really be mine?

The champagne-colored couture gown's lace bodice accentuated her breasts, showing ample cleavage. The straps covered her perfect shoulders, blending with her flawless complexion. The floor-length gown flared outward from her knees gently touching the floor and the matching Jimmy Choo designer heels.

Hand-made lace covered the satin-bodiced, hip-hugging flared dress. Layers of tulle with an overall diamante pattern covered the entire dress, causing the entire outfit to shimmer and sparkle as she moved.

Oh WOW! She was so used to wearing simple navy scrubs that getting dressed up was something special.

"Let me do your makeup for you," her friend offered. Madison knew better than to argue with Lexie, who pretty much always got her own way. Lexie gently worked some foundation into Madison's already flawless complexion. She added the slightest amount of blush to accentuate her cheekbones and blended eyeshadow to complement the designer dress, making Madison's emerald green almond-shaped eyes stand out even more. Gently applying mascara, Lexie wondered how anyone could possibly have such long eyelashes without using extensions.

"Before we add your lipstick, let's crack open the bottle of champagne that's been chilling here." Before Madison had time to comment, the cork flew off the bottle of bubbly and Lexie was pouring two flutes of Dom Perignon.

"Cheers! Here's looking at you kid." Lexie proclaimed as she handed Madison one of the flutes.

The guests would soon be arriving, and Madison still needed to finalize the items for the auction with the museum representative and the auctioneer.

Downing the flute of champagne, which was really sacrilege given that it was Dom Perignon, Madison grabbed her matching purse, hitched up the bottom of her ball gown and was about to leave the suite when Lexie shouted after her.

"Hey Madison! Aren't you forgetting the most important thing?" Madison looked at her quizzically.

"Oh yes, my mask—thanks for reminding me. Seriously Lexie, I don't know what I would do without you. Please, could you help me with the ribbons?"

Lexie held the intricately adorned champagne-colored filigree mask with diamante detail that matched her dress perfectly. She gently tied the ribbons behind Madison's hair, hiding them under the curls that cascaded down her bare back.

"There you go! All I can say is that you look absolutely perfect. Go knock 'em dead girlfriend!" Lexie realized that Madison was likely to be schmoozing with the rich and famous for the rest of the night. She was proud of best friend. Madison worked relentlessly and if ever someone deserved a special night off, it was her.

Stepping into the museum was like being transported to a magical fairytale. The entire venue had been transformed with thousands upon thousands of lights suspended from the high ceiling. Fresh flowers were everywhere. At least 50 tables were comfortably spaced with place settings arranged for 500 people. Table centerpieces adorned each table on top of floor-length brocade tablecloths. Each place setting had an individual name card as well as a printed five-course menu.

Can this really all be happening for me this evening? Everything is simply perfect. I hope that we make our target tonight. What the heck, let's go and have some fun!

Surveying the museum, Madison suddenly realized she hadn't felt this excited for... well, maybe she'd never quite been this excited about anything before.

Brad

The cabin attendant walked down the aisle of the Gulfstream jet toward its lone passenger.

"We're about 10 to 15 minutes out, Mr. Anderson."

"Thanks, Edward," Brad Anderson answered as he shut down his laptop. He began getting ready for the descent into the Baltimore/Washington International Airport. As the jet taxied on the runway, 34-year-old Brad reached for his leather dual purpose travel bag. Checking his Rolex, he should have enough time to get to the Four Seasons, shower and get ready for this fundraiser.

Standing up, he stretched his 6-foot frame and reached for his iPhone. His casual shirt did nothing to cover his broad shoulders and muscular arms, and his tailored pants looked as though they were designed specifically for him—which they were.

"Hey Steve, I've just landed. Can I patch you through to the pilot so you can bring the car around?"

Brad is always the consummate professional. He must be. As partner and CEO of one of the largest tech firms in Palo Alto, Silicon Valley, he is the face of the business. He never knows when a journalist may recognize him and ambush him for an interview.

This is the reason for the jet. Not that Brad minds the comfort and luxury. It's been years since he last flew on a commercial vessel and it's not likely to happen again anytime soon. As the Gulfstream comes to a halt, he notices that Steve is already waiting for him.

"I should be done by around 11:00 this evening Edward. Please, could you arrange that we're refueled and ready for takeoff as close to then as possible?"

"Sure. Will do Mr. Anderson."

Brad can't stand wasting even one minute of time because for him, time is money. If there's one thing that he won't tolerate, it is lack of productivity. If this dinner was for anything other than neurology, he would have declined the invitation. His dad died from a brain tumor that could have possibly been operated on, had the technology existed at the time. This made this cause very close to his heart.

Brad handed his bag to Steve as he climbed into the back of the luxury car with his laptop.

"Four Seasons?"

"Yes please, Steve! You know me too well. I'm going to have to find another favorite venue in Baltimore just to keep you on your toes." Brad teases. And that's it, end of conversation. Steve knows Brad is now back in what he refers to as "the zone." Steve has never met another professional quite like Brad. He's not surprised that Brad is still a bachelor, as he's dedicated to his job to the point where he hardly has any social life. This is one of the few times Steve has ever known Brad to attend a social function in Baltimore.

"We're here, Mr. Anderson."

"Thanks Steve. Can you be back here to fetch me at 7:00 this evening? I believe that the museum's not too far from here."

"Will do, Mr. Anderson. It will probably take us about 15 minutes to get there."

"That's great, Steve. Thanks again. I'll see you later." Brad took his bag from Steve and headed toward the reception area.

"Good afternoon, Mr. Anderson. Welcome back to the Four Seasons. Your suite is all ready for you!" Brad collected the keys for the suite he usually stays in whenever he's in Baltimore. He prefers the space of a suite where he can work and hold meetings if need be. Tonight is all about the fundraiser though. He's more than a little annoyed that his business partner, Donovan Brown, wasn't quite comfortable facing a crowd of people, not even for a cause such as this one. At least he gave Brad carte blanche when it came to what he was allowed to donate to the hospital.

Unzipping his bag, Brad unpacked his tuxedo, shirt, and bowtie. There was enough time to shower before meeting Steve downstairs.

Brad climbed into the oversized shower, set the water temperature and allowed the steady flow of the water jets to spray against his tanned, muscular body. It was on occasions like this, that he wished he had someone special to share the moments with. As quickly as he thought about it, he dismissed himself.

You've had plenty of chances at romance, probably more than most. And what have you done with every opportunity? Absolutely nothing!

Not that any of the relationships he was famous for were with anyone worth settling down with. It seemed that he was able to find plenty of Ms. Right Now's without being able to find Ms. Right. He'd actually given up on love completely and decided he was destined to be a bachelor for the rest of his life.

With the kind of bank balance he had, there were always women falling all over him. It was something that he really had an issue with. Would he ever meet someone who could appreciate him for who he was, without having to worry about how much he was worth (which was a small fortune)? Did such a woman exist? Lost in thought, Brad dressed as though he were on autopilot. Splashing his face with Clive Christian No.1, he was almost ready to head downstairs. One last thing—this is a masked ball. His plain black mask fit snugly over his chiseled nose. The one thing it couldn't do was hide the ice-blue eyes behind it.

Brad was pleasantly surprised by the way the museum had been decorated for the evening. It was a romantic setting. He pondered again, if only there were someone he could share the evening with. The table he was sitting at was a bit of a mixed bag with some prestigious doctors from Johns Hopkins, investment bankers, and from the conversation, he could only guess real estate developers.

There were a lot of things auctioned off by the museum that had been donated to the main cause. The evening gave him some time to unwind after several extremely busy months where his company had successfully completed several acquisitions that would prove to be extremely lucrative for their business.

Brad wasn't interested in bidding on anything, but he wanted to make a sizable donation to the hospital. Calling one of the server's over, he quietly asked them how he could go about donating by check.

They excused themselves for a few minutes and returned with an empty envelope and tacky-looking pen from the museum. Brad hauled out his checkbook and his Mont Blanc pen. Writing out the check and countersigning alongside Donovan's signature, he gave the ink a few moments to dry before sealing it in the envelope and placing the envelope back on the tray.

Brad was getting ready to leave when he noticed where the server was going.

Across the room from him stood the most exquisite creature he'd ever laid eyes on. She was tiny, yet gorgeous, wearing one of the most beautiful dresses he had ever seen. Her skin reminded him of peaches and cream and was flawless. Behind the mask, all he could see was a most mesmerizing pair of emerald green eyes. She had a perfectly oval face with raven-colored hair, professionally styled with locks running halfway down her backless gown.

Handing the envelope to Madison, the server motioned in Brad's direction. For a few moments, their eyes met, and it was as though the entire museum stood still.

He held her gaze for as long as he could before she looked down to open the envelope. Brad suddenly felt as if his heart would beat out of his chest. He could hardly breathe and needed to get outside. Those eyes! There was something vaguely familiar about them. Leaving, Brad was convinced he imagined the instant connection between him and the green-eyed beauty.

Madison gasped at the number of zeros on the check she was holding in her hands. Looking up, all she saw was Brad's wide back as he moved quickly out of the room. She felt a mixture of emotions all at once; curiosity, disappointment, and desire all rolled into one.

Chapter 2: In My Dreams

Brad

"Steve, I'm done a bit earlier than expected." Brad's voice was raspy and he could still feel his heart beating in his throat. "I'll be waiting outside the main entrance for you." Desperately trying to catch his breath, he tugged at the bowtie, loosening the top button of his white shirt in a futile attempt to relieve the pressure. The way he was breathing, he felt as though he'd just completed the Boston Marathon!

Get it together Brad. What the hell's wrong with you? Geez, you're behaving like a schoolboy with his first CRUSH! What makes you think she even noticed you? She was clearly more interested in the number on the check. Those eyes though! I could get lost in them forever.

Brad was immediately brought back to reality as Steve pulled up and opened the door for him.

"How was the dinner, Mr. Anderson?" Steve asked, in his usual chatty tone. When he received no answer, he decided not to press the subject. This made two things stand out on this trip; he'd never known Brad to really unwind, and from the look of it, something had definitely happened at the dinner.

Brad was still completely at a loss for words. He had never felt such an immediate attraction to someone before. Even though there were several tables between them, he took in almost everything about her. Part of his career involved summing people up within the first few seconds of meeting them and his gut had never failed him.

What is her story though? Where is she from? Who is she? Part of the museum? Maybe she is an event planner, hired to oversee arrangements for the evening? How will I ever find her again?

There was no way he was going to leave it there. Brad simply had too many questions and very few answers. He'd had dated many gorgeous women, usually a different one for every function or event he attended and yet, had never felt such an immediate, magnetic attraction in his life!

Did I just imagine what happened there tonight? Was the chemistry mutual? That's never happened in… ever!

Brad's mind was swirling with too many questions and not enough answers by the time Steve pulled up next to the Gulfstream. Opening the door for Brad, he was still oddly puzzled by Brad's demeanor. It was as though something had unnerved him—something that in all the years Steve had worked for Brad Anderson had simply never happened. Brad was always as cool as anything and totally professional.

Grabbing his luggage from Steve, he mumbled, "Thanks, Steve. See you when I'm next in town." and left it at that! Edward was waiting at the bottom of the stairs ready to take Brad's bag.

"We're just waiting for clearance from the control tower, but we should be able to take off by 11:00 p.m. as you requested," Edward was telling Brad.

"Uh huh," was the sum total of what Edward received in response.

What's up with Mr. Anderson? He's usually very professional, but tonight he seems completely aloof. His head is clearly elsewhere. I hope he doesn't have food poisoning or something. That would make for an interesting flight!

True to his word, the jet was cleared for takeoff at exactly 11:00 p.m. and began to slowly taxi down one of the long runways heading out of the Baltimore/Washington Airport.

Brad was slowly beginning to feel as though his breathing was returning to normal. For a moment there he thought, *I may need to call a doctor to meet us at the San Jose Airport.*

By the time the jet started to climb, he was sitting a bit more comfortably on one of the plush white leather seats that were custom detailed when Brown, Anderson & Associates purchased the jet. He'd removed his tuxedo jacket, leaving the bowtie slightly loose around his neck. In his hands he was toying with the black mask he'd worn to the dinner.

Feeling more composed finally, he asked Edward to pour him a drink.

"What's your poison tonight, Mr. Anderson? Dom Perignon, Glenfiddich, or Johnnie Walker Blue?" Edward stood ready for Brad's choice.

"Make it a double Johnnie Walker on the rocks, Edward."

Brad was still trying to come to terms with his last few minutes at the museum, so maybe a stiff drink would sort them out?

Returning with a crystal whiskey glass on a silver tray, Edward commented that their flying time to San Jose Airport would be approximately another 5 hours or so.

"Thanks Edward. I think I'll try and get a few more hours' work in." As he took his first sip of his favorite scotch, Brad finally placed the mask on the table next to him. Powering up his laptop, he had a ton of work he knew was waiting for him that needed to be addressed urgently, as usual.

Opening his emails, he picked up a mail from Donovan checking in on the fundraiser. Brad quickly dropped him a response that would automatically be sent the moment they landed in San Jose when he changed from "in flight" mode.

Many business executives became frustrated with being out of contact for so long during lengthy flights. Brad sees it as a bit of downtime where he can complete presentations, respond to emails, and generally get a lot of admin done.

He began typing his response to Donovan telling him about the vixen that he'd shared a moment with across the museum floor. Reading over what he wrote brought only one word to mind; *'Cheesy!'*

Your partner obviously wants to know how many zeros you dropped at this dinner this evening and you're carrying on like a lovesick puppy dog. Nice one, Brad! Get with the program. Your chances of ever meeting up with her again probably match the number of zeros on the check... without the first digit!

Getting back to the email to Donovan, he sat backspacing to delete the account of the momentary glance that had turned his whole world upside down.

Just thinking about her sent Brad's mind all over the place. He couldn't stop himself from imagining running one of his fingers gently from her neck, down to her shoulders and all the way down her arm. He just knows that her skin would feel like silk. That complexion was absolutely flawless.

Desperately trying to snap back to the present moment, Brad found that fighting his emotions proved to be a hopeless endeavor. Deciding that his efforts to work were useless, he snapped his laptop shut. Returning it to his briefcase, he decides to try and get a couple of hours of shut eye before another busy day.

He motioned for Edward to bring him a blanket while downing the last of the amber liquid in his glass.

"Goodnight, Mr. Anderson. I'm here if you need anything." Edward replied while ensuring that the glass was removed, and Brad had everything else he needed. Noticing that Brad had kicked off his formal Polo shoes, Edward thought *the one thing he seemed to be holding onto was that black mask. Strange.*

No sooner had Brad started dozing off when his imagination returned to him holding the raven-haired beauty close to him. He could imagine that she smelled like his favorite perfume, Joy Baccarat, Limited Edition, with its strong leanings toward jasmine and rose.

He wanted to know what it felt like to press his lips on the back of her neck. What was hiding behind that intricate delicate mask she was wearing, he wondered? He found himself dreaming of different scenarios where they were together, enjoying the wind blowing through those raven-colored locks as he drove her to his home in Palo Alto.

Forcing himself awake, Brad realized that until he knew who this woman was, he was quite possibly going to prove totally useless to anyone and everyone around him. He'd already spent way too much time thinking about her, which was totally out of character.

Glancing at his Rolex, he realized that they'd soon be landing at San Jose Airport where his car was parked. Anything to keep his mind from wandering would be a relief, rather than feeling like a foolish schoolboy back in high school!

Greeting the flight crew as they touched down at San Jose, he double-checked that he had everything before disembarking. *I can't leave this behind,* he thought, grabbing the black mask from the table.

It's the only thing he had to remind him of last night's events at the museum. Donning his tuxedo jacket, he reached into his pocket to stash the mask when he suddenly discovered the printed name tag from the dinner. He must have slipped it into his pocket together with his checkbook.

Starting his silver Lexus LC, he was looking forward to the drive home. It would hopefully get his mind off of her!

Madison

It was 1:30 a.m. before Lexie and Madison finally walked back into Madison's waterfront apartment. Walked was possibly the wrong word, as Madison, though completely exhausted, was floating as if on her very own cloud.

"I simply couldn't have asked for a more perfect evening, Lexie!" Madison was almost giddy, and Lexie wasn't sure whether this was an aftereffect of too much Dom Perignon, or the amount of money that had been raised.

"I must get out of these shoes; they've been pinching my toes together almost the whole evening and I feel like I have lockjaw from smiling so much. If I had to smile for one more photograph, I think my face would stay that way permanently!" Madison kicked off the Jimmy Choo heels and tried to gently massage her feet.

Lexie was one of the few people who Madison was totally comfortable with, partly because they'd been best friends since Columbia University and partly because their lives had remained intertwined with both being accepted at Johns Hopkins.

While many of Madison and David's mutual friends had chosen to stick with David, it was pretty much just Lexie who had convinced Madison to cut the cord. David had put up a fuss when the divorce papers were finally served to him, trying his best to play on Madison's incredibly soft nature. Thank goodness Lexie was like a voice of reason. She stuck by Madison through thick and thin, especially when all her other so-called friends were abandoning her like rats off a sinking ship.

Alexa James heritage was a combination of Italian and American, which often accounted for her volatile personality. Not that she was always like that; it depended on who you were and whether she liked you or not. Thank goodness Madison fell under the 'like' category. She had once witnessed one of Alexa's full-blown Italian rants and all she could say was that she felt sorry for the person on the receiving end.

Madison had always called her *Lexie* as a term of endearment, even from their early days at Columbia. She was of average height and build with an olive complexion, dark brown eyes, and a mop of dark brown hair that seldom cooperated with her, especially under a surgical scrub cap. She chose pediatrics as her specialty and got to wear pink scrubs.

Hoping to cheer up the older children, she was often seen wearing brightly-colored scrub caps with comical patterns and designs on them. That was just how Lexie was. It was one of the things that Madison loved about her friend.

When Madison chose to join Johns Hopkins as an intern, Lexie applied simply to be close to her friend. Little did she know that she would be accepted.

Lexie immediately went to the refrigerator for the bottle of freshly squeezed orange juice. Out from under her jacket came a sealed bottle of Dom Perignon.

"What?" she asked Madison, responding to the quizzical look on her face. "There were a couple of extra bottles left over and there's no way I was going to let them go to waste!"

"Lexie, didn't you have enough throughout the evening?" Madison asked, although she knew the answer that was likely to come right back at her.

"Well, you were busy entertaining all the snobs, so somebody had to have some fun!"

"I'm so sorry that you couldn't be with me, my friend. You can be grateful. Performing an 18-hour surgical procedure has absolutely nothing on trying to stand in Jimmy Choo's for a couple of hours! Give me my surgical clogs any day." Madison laughed.

"So...? Tell me about this mystery man who donated all the cash." Lexie was never one to back down from trying to set Madison up with Mr. Right.

"What do you mean by mystery man? I just happened to make eye contact with him from across the room." Madison's voice sounded fake to Lexie.

"And...? Come on Madison, I know you better than you know yourself. Spill the beans!"

Lexie was relentless and Madison knew she wasn't likely to get out of telling her everything that she wasn't even sure was real.

"Pour me a Mimosa and I'll tell you everything." Madison went on to recount the server bringing an envelope which he said was from the gentleman at table 15. When asked who this gentleman was, the server pointed him out to her.

"Lexie, our eyes met, and it was like everything else melted into the background, I thought I was going to fall over if I kept looking at him. So, I did the next best thing and looked at the envelope." Madison continued, "I swear, Lexie... That man's ice-blue eyes could see right through me and into my soul!"

"And...?" Lexie knew just how to keep a conversation going.

"There was a check for $2,000,000 in the envelope from an offshore account. I could only make out one of the signatures on the check. It looked like the surname was Brown. When I looked up to go over and thank him, all that I saw was the back of him as he left the museum."

"So, what did he look like?" Lexie pressed Madison for more information.

"It's hard to say really... From what I saw, he was quite tall, and extremely well built." Madison stopped for a minute to sip some of her Mimosa. "I didn't really get a good look at him. Most of his face was covered by a black mask that seemed as though it was custom made for him. He had blonde hair and was extremely well dressed, as in professional-tailor well dressed!”

“I thought you said you didn't get a good look at him, girlfriend? That sounds like a pretty good look to me!” Lexie good-naturedly chided her best friend.

“The problem is that I have absolutely no idea who he was. I mean, seriously Lexie, who comes to a fundraising auction and doesn't buy anything? Instead, he simply wrote out a check that could cover almost the whole production in one go. Who has that kind of money?”

“Well, you're lucky I didn't see him first,” Lexie teased. “You know my theory on men with large checkbooks—overcompensating!”

Madison knew exactly what Lexie was referring to, as that was the typical modus operandi of her ex, David. He'd flash some money around only to have all the plastic bimbos in the area swooning over him. Boy, was she glad to be rid of him and their toxic marriage!

“The weird thing about this guy Lexie, was that when I went to the table where he was sitting, his place card was missing. How will I ever find him to thank him for his huge donation?”

“Are you sure that's the reason you're trying to find him—Mr. Prince Charming? Madison's got a CRUSH!” Lexie accused, continuing to tease her friend.

“Oh, shut up Lexie.” Madison threw a throw cushion in Lexie's general direction. “Come and help me out of this gown. I'm absolutely exhausted and it's seriously late.” Madison grabbed her Mimosa and headed toward her bedroom with Lexie hot on her heels.

"Lexie, I don't want you trying to drive home, so please sleep in the guest bedroom. Thank goodness we're both off today because I don't think I could have faced pulling a shift after all the excitement from last night. I still can't believe that we managed to raise almost $10,000,000!" Madison exclaimed, while stifling a yawn.

"I'm going to jump in the shower quickly Madison, but yeah, I'll stay over. I'm also feeling really tired all of a sudden. See you a bit later, my darling friend! I'm really so proud of you. I knew you could do it. Your new program is going to revolutionize the way the hospital approaches neurology." Lexie wandered down to the guest bedroom leaving her friend to get ready for bed.

Before removing her ball gown, Madison did one final twirl and was fascinated by the way it shimmered as the light caught each tiny diamante that had been hand sewn into the gown.

Slipping into her satin pajamas, she sat in front of her bedroom mirror armed with facial cleanser and toner to remove her makeup. This was the worst part of all the fancy dinners and banquets. Normally, Madison wore only the faintest shade of lipstick or a bit of gloss. She hated having to do the whole cleansing routine.

Climbing into bed, Madison stared up at the ceiling. She was exhausted, but unable to fall asleep. All she could focus on was the memory of those ice-blue eyes.

How am I supposed to find out who the mystery man is? There's no way I'll be able to sleep tonight until I figure it out. Madison, there are over 2,500,000 people living in the Baltimore area. It's going to be like looking for a needle in a haystack.

Turning on her side, Madison tried to fall asleep, and got the same result as before—the memory of ice-blue eyes!

Chapter 3: Searching

Madison

"Somebody switch that off and let me die in peace, please!" Ranting at her alarm clock, Madison was feeling the aftereffects of the night before. She pulled the oversized goose-down pillow over her head. "That last Mimosa you forced me to drink with you last night really did it, Lexie. This is all your fault."

"Good morning sunshine!" Lexie's typical cheerfulness was almost annoying at that point. "Drink this and you'll be back to your normal self in no time at all."

"Argh, Lexie, two Tylenol's just aren't going to do it for me this morning and I'm on call today..." Madison peered out from beneath the pillow. "How come you never seem to suffer from hangovers no matter how much you have to drink?"

"It must be my Italian side coming out. Oh, and I made sure I had something to eat before leaving the hospital yesterday."

"Thanks for the heads up on that one... You didn't think of getting me anything? Some best friend you are." Madison's legs dangled off the bed as she tried to force herself into motion. She climbed into the shower to wake up and wash the hairspray out of her hair from the night before. The heat from the shower jets pulsated all over her body. She began feeling slightly more awake than she had a few minutes ago. Lathering soap all over her tiny frame, she felt an immediate sense of relief from her aching muscles.

Letting her mind wander, her thoughts betrayed her, catching her off-guard, as she was transported back to that singular brief encounter from the night before. Could she really have imagined the magnetic attraction between her and the mystery man?

I'd love to know what was really under that mask, under that tailor-made tuxedo, and more importantly, behind those eyes... If only he were here right now, I would just melt into his arms. What I wouldn't give to have those arms around me right now, pulling me closer. What would it be like to have him with me in the shower this morning? His caress would be gentle, yet firm, at the same time. What would his kisses taste like? Whimpering, she realized she was beginning to drive herself insane thinking about this guy.

How could someone she'd never even met have such a powerful effect on her? How was she ever going to find him? Wrapping herself in a towel, she joined Lexie. Not wanting to answer any more questions, she chose to keep the provocative thoughts of her mystery man to herself. Pulling on her scrubs and clogs, she combed her long, black hair into a ponytail, ready to face whatever was coming her way.

"Is there time for Starbucks on the way in? I'm starving this morning," Lexie asked.

Rounding the corner to the hospital, Madison's phone began to buzz. The ring tone showed that it was an emergency and she was needed. Regaining her composure, she sat upright, maneuvering the car into the hospital parking lot. "Sorry Lexie, we'll have to send out for coffee and breakfast this morning."

"Thank goodness I have a spare set of scrubs in my locker! Maybe it's time I leave a set of scrubs at your apartment too." Lexie said with a grin.

Heading to Neurology, Madison couldn't stop thinking about her mystery man. *Once I'm done with this emergency, I need to figure out a way of finding Mr. Blue Eyes.*

Stop it now Madison! It's time to come back to the real world—there are people relying on you to save their lives. You're behaving like a love-sick schoolgirl! The last time you were so head-over-heels in love was with that senior, Brad Anderson, back at Huntington Beach High School, and we all know how that turned out.

He didn't even know you existed with your scruffy haircut and hand-me-down clothes. He was more interested in the cheerleader and homecoming queen, Bethany Roberts. It's time to pull yourself together and to focus.

Returning to the doctors' lounge after surgery, Madison powered up her laptop and began a search at the one place she knew that Mr. Blue Eyes had been—the fundraising dinner at the art museum last night. Scanning the celebrity and media pages, Madison was not surprised to find her face and name staring back at her from every major Baltimore news publication. It also reported an undisclosed sum of money donated by an anonymous organization.

Annoyed that the donation had been leaked to the media, Madison turned her attention to additional media footage from the event. Scanning each photograph, there was only one photograph that looked remotely like it may have been a partial image of her mystery man. No further information. The caption below simply read 'guests.'

Well, this is completely hopeless; I'm already hitting a brick wall. Maybe I should just forget about him and try to get some work done.

Resigning herself to the fact that she would probably never see him again, Madison turned her attention to her emails.

Brad

Driving home along the winding coastline of Palo Alto, Brad was trying to concentrate on the road in front of him. He adjusted his Bentley Platinum shades to cut the glare of early morning sunrise beginning to greet the Pacific coast. He'd driven this same road so many times that his convertible should have known its own way home by now.

His thoughts were interrupted by the events of the previous evening. *Why can't I get that woman out of my head? She's going to drive me crazy until I know exactly who she is and how to find her again. Once I've wrapped up this Tokyo deal, I can spend the rest of the day playing detective.* A wry smile crossed his lips.

There was also the matter of a faint hint of stubble that he'd have to deal with once he got home. He looked forward to getting out of his tux and into something a bit more comfortable. Turning into Westminster Drive and travelling a few blocks along it, Brad pressed the remote for the main gates of the mansion he'd been living in for the last seven years to open. He'd imagined that the four spare bedrooms would be occupied by his children by this time. He came to the sad realization that it was not going to happen anytime soon either.

The only company he had when he was at home was his gardener, Ruiz, and the housekeeper, Maria. They had both worked for him ever since he settled in Palo Alto more than a decade ago.

Quickly slipping into the shower before his conference call, he tried his best to soak away the memories of "the gallery vixen." Not having much luck, his thoughts began racing again and he felt himself wanting her near him... he imagined unzipping that magnificent champagne gown that was clearly designed for her... there would be nothing to see but her bare back as he gently lifted the straps from her perfectly shaped shoulders.

He imagined her standing in front of him naked, except for her shoes and maybe some sexy lace pull-up stockings. He imagined every single detail of her frame by frame, until each of the images was seared into his brain forever.

Wrapping his towel around his waist, Brad surveyed the contents of his walk-in-closet. He decided on a pair of khaki chinos and a powder-blue Lacoste golf shirt. Fortunately, the meeting wasn't going to be a long, or very formal one.

Settling into his study, Brad notified Tokyo that he was standing by and ready whenever they were. Reaching a positive conclusion to the meeting some 45 minutes later, he was pleased to be returning to his real mission for the day.

Deciding where to look first wasn't too difficult or challenging. He'd noticed that there was plenty of press and media at the event and was certain that someone, somewhere, would have mentioned the catering service or event planning company she represented. While she was the most gorgeous attraction at the whole dinner, he'd already resigned himself that she was hired help, or a curator at the museum at best. Chances were that someone knew exactly who she was.

Scrolling through the Baltimore media headlines of the day, there were loads of articles surrounding the dinner, especially one about an anonymous donation of $2,000,000 minus an auction bid or purchase. Brad just smiled.

With one more click, there she was staring back at him! The exact same piercing emerald-green eyes were on his screen. But hang on; she's nowhere near the help. This was her event! It was Dr. Madison Watson, the top neurologist at Johns Hopkins. It was her program that he'd specifically travelled from the west coast to the east coast to attend.

How could he have not known who she was? *How do I contact her now so that I don't look like I'm actually stalking her? Facebook request? Nah, too tacky and I doubt she's even on Facebook.*

LinkedIn may be a bit more professional. So, what do I say to her? Hi, remember me? I'm the one who gave you the big, fat check before running out of there like a little schoolboy. By the way, would you like to have dinner some time?

What's to say she's not already married, Brad? You're busy spacing yourself out over some woman you'll probably never see again, and you're worried about how to ask her on a date? What's wrong with you?

Nothing but the best was good enough for Brad, but he remembered his humble beginnings at Huntington High School. He'd come a long way since then, thanks to his business partner, Donovan Brown. Donovan was not one for being directly in the public eye. He was more like a wizard behind the curtain performing the magic of the tech business. Brad had met Donovan at Stanford. Quite an unusual bond had formed between them. Donovan was known as a typical tech geek, while Brad was a business major. By the time they'd both qualified, he was the only person Donovan trusted with the day-to-day handling of his business.

Brad, on the other hand, was what you'd call the front man of the business. Handling negotiations, attending meetings and being the face of Brown, Anderson & Associates was what he lived for. He'd never married or found anyone suitable for any kind of long-term relationship. Sure, he'd had more than his fair share of short-term relationships, but they all ended the same way. None of the prospects were marriage material. None of them could really hold an intelligent conversation. All they were really good for was an evening of fun and having a bit of eye candy on his arm.

Brad's biggest fear was that he'd end up single for the rest of his life. If he was honest with himself, he was lonely in his large luxury home. It was the kind of home that had all the amenities anyone could hope for, but he needed someone to share it with.

All the women he had dated over the years could never understand his total commitment to his work. They never understood his vision to retire by the time he was 45. His dream was to travel the world and share it with someone who'd be able to enjoy it with him.

Madison and David

Madison had her reasons for erring on the side of caution when it came to men. *Never again will I allow some man to completely dominate me. I'll take my time playing the same games as they do, even if it means having a few Mr. Right Now's while searching for my Mr. Right!*

This thinking was totally opposite to everything Madison stood for, but the scars left by David were going to take a long time to heal. There was no way she'd be jumping into any long-term relationship following her sham of a marriage to David. Four years of marriage had been four years too long for Madison. The affairs had started shortly after they'd said, "I do," as far as Madison knew, and this was enough to make her wary of relationships altogether.

Lexie, however, knew the whole sordid truth about David, which is why she loathed him so. They had all been friends at Columbia together while studying medicine. David was a no-good cheater then and nothing had changed. She'd tried to warn Madison about him, but David would always respond with some lie-filled story and Madison was so blinded by his charms that she'd always believed him.

David professed to be her 'soulmate' and they were almost always together. He was the one person who knew Madison from when she first arrived at Columbia University looking like the geeky dork that left Huntington Beach. The truth behind David was that he'd been dared by his Delta Kappa fraternity brothers to find the ugliest girl at their beginning of the year party, pursue said girl for the first semester, and then dump her by the end of the semester. In David's books, Madison was the only prospect for him to receive the coveted Delta Kappa Trophy at the beginning of the second semester.

Madison was still wearing braces, her hair could hardly be classified as styled and she was not the most up-to-date in the fashion department. Lexie being Lexie always seemed to blend in with the crowd and got wind of what the Delta Kappa brothers were doing. She was immediately drawn to Madison, who then became her "pet project" for the rest of the semester.

Thanks to Lexie, Madison could finally break out of the shell that had held her captive throughout high school. Her deadbeat dad had left her and her mom high and dry in Huntington with no money and no means of financial support. Heather Watson had worked three jobs just to try to keep food on the table and a roof over their heads.

Madison's braces had cost what seemed like a fortune and Heather could only afford to buy second-hand clothes from the clothing bank. Most of them hung like flour sacks on Madison's tiny frame. There was nothing glamorous or stylish about any of them, but Madison appreciated what her mother was trying to do for her.

Chapter 4: Columbia

Mr. Carmichael

She never told her mother about the way she was treated at school and how she'd spent most of her time studying between the library and Mr. Carmichael's laboratory. The laboratory was the only place she really felt at home, working with physics and chemistry. Mr. Carmichael, the physics and chemistry grades head, would allow her into the lab before school and after school. He knew that she was passionate about his subjects and saw great potential in her.

He had been the one to suggest that she submit college applications to various universities where she'd be able to study medicine. He had written glowing references to the point where she'd been offered a full-ride scholarship at Columbia. Forever grateful to "Mr. C." as she affectionately referred to him, she appreciated that, without his references, she would have been forced to settle for a job at the local diner, just as her mother had done.

Her deadbeat dad couldn't be found to pay child support and Madison was used to being a charity case. She became a loner, preferring her own company and getting lost in her own world of physics and chemistry. Acceptance at Columbia could make all the difference to her life. All she needed to do was to maintain a 3.75 grade point average.

Alexa James

Lexie became fascinated with the tiny little wallflower who really had no idea what was happening in the world around her. She was so soft and good natured, which made her an easy target, especially for the bunch of immature creeps at Delta Kappa. There was no way she was going to let David Webb have his way with Madison.

Lexie installed herself directly into Madison's life by planning with Admissions that she and Madison would end up sharing a room together. Her main mission (apart from getting her degree) was going to be to transform Madison.

Operation 1 - Time for the braces to go…

"Madison, don't make any arrangements after Psych 101 today!"

"Why?" Madison asked in her soft-spoken tone. "Do you want me to help you with your physics again today?"

"No! I've got something way cooler planned for you—whatever you do, dress comfortably, we're going to have to walk all the way to one of the other main admin blocks."

"Whatever for?"

"Don't you worry—just you wait and see. I promise it will all be worth it." Madison had learned not to ask too many questions when it came to Alexa James. She was probably the coolest dorm roommate in the whole of Columbia. Crazy as hell, but Madison knew that for the first time in her life, she had someone in her corner whom she could trust.

True to form, at the end of the day, Lexie was waiting for Madison outside the Psych lecture hall. Lexie always seemed to be waiting for Madison everywhere, but that's what a sidekick does. Heading into the dentistry wing of the university, Madison suddenly became tense.

"No Lexie, you didn't!"

"Oh, yes I did."

About an hour later, with much clenching of armrests, rinsing and spitting, and rinsing some more, she was shown the result of the last five years of her life wearing braces. She had perfectly straight, perfectly white teeth and no longer had to cover her mouth nervously to hide a smile.

"Oh Lexie, how can I ever repay you for what you've done?"

"But I'm just getting started, Madison. Wait until you see what I have in store for you tomorrow. And, there's absolutely no payment necessary. Just to see the look on your face is payment enough for me."

Madison virtually bounced all the way back to their dorm smiling broadly at anyone and everyone. She was so proud of the way her teeth had turned out that the five years of agonizing torture by the local orthodontist in Huntington Beach began to fade away into the distance.

<u>Operation 2 - The Mop</u>

The following day, Madison woke to find Lexie already up and about. It was a Saturday, which meant no classes, but there were usually socials happening everywhere on campus. Lexie had specifically told Madison to keep the day open, which she duly did.

"Come on girlfriend. We've got some retail therapy ahead of us today!"

"But Lexie, I don't have any money to spend frivolously on whatever I want."

"No, no, no, I insist. This is my treat. There's a reason why I have a Platinum Card from Daddy! It's for moments exactly like this. Besides, I've hardly charged anything since the semester began. First stop, the hairdresser!"

Madison couldn't remember ever being at a hairdresser before. She nervously sat down on one of the hairdressing chairs, sheepishly looking at herself through what could only be described as an unruly mop of hair.

"Morning ladies. What are we doing with this hair today?" The hairdresser seemed to approach Madison's hair as a monumental challenge so early in the morning.

"I need you to make her look absolutely gorgeous," Alexa instructed.

This is going to take a HUGE miracle this morning, the hairdresser mused, directing Madison to the wash basins. Working her magic on Madison's hair was actually a bit easier than she thought it would be, massaging it with oils to counteract the dry, brittle texture of her raven-black hair. Next, came the fine gold hairdressing scissors and within half an hour, Madison could not believe the transformation.

The only way to salvage her unruly mop of hair was to layer it into a shoulder-length style with a slight fringe to the side. Instead of peering out from behind her hair, suddenly Madison's perfectly oval face was open, surrounded by her dark hair, revealing the most exquisite emerald green eyes that were almond shaped with eyelashes to die for.

"Oh wow! I knew there was someone under there. Moving on to the next phase."

Operation 3 - Retail Therapy

"Let's hit some boutiques to find you some decent threads, and then my job here is done!" Linking arms together, Lexie and Madison began visiting all the trendy little shops all over the Big Apple. Lexie seemed to know exactly where to go for all the best deals. Almost the entire day was spent trying on different outfits which either received a triumphant thumbs-up sign, or a definite thumb down.

Lexie had a way of scrunching up her nose and shaking her head whenever it was a negative. By lunchtime, they'd run up some serious coin on Lexie's father's Platinum card. Madison was totally overwhelmed by it all and was a little teary-eyed as they headed toward Brownie's Café back on campus.

Nobody had ever done anything like this for her! She was so used to being the wallflower with the "hand-me-down-hang-like-a-sack" clothes that her mother bought from all the charity shops, that she'd never owned anything new since her father left them for a younger woman when Madison was just 10 years old.

Lexie still wasn't quite done with Madison. They'd been invited to a mixer at Delta Kappa by David that evening. Lexie insisted that Madison wear one of the coolest outfits they'd bought that day and touched up her makeup ever so slightly.

Now to see the expression on David Webb's face! Lexie thought.

If there was one thing that Lexie knew how to do, it was to make a grand entrance and, on this occasion, the grander the better. The last thing Lexie wanted to do was to hurt Madison, or see her hurt, which was the only outcome she could foresee where David Webb was involved.

He had a typical bad-boy reputation and was unlikely to change. The challenge at Delta Kappa was not going to be won by David! Entering the main entrance to the fraternity house, the girls could see that the mixer was already in full swing. The moment that Lexie saw David, she knew that the house was exactly where they needed to be.

Seeing Lexie, David was about to ask where Madison was, when he must have figured out that the vixen standing next to Lexie was, in fact, Madison, who had been transformed from an ugly duckling into a beautiful swan.

"Madison, you look great..." stammered David. It was all he managed to get out. He could hardly believe his eyes and knew from that moment that he absolutely had to have her. David never won the trophy for the frat boy with the ugliest girl by the end of the first semester. Not to say that Lexie made life easy for him. She knew all about his type, plus there were rumors on campus that he was a bit of a player and chased after every piece of skirt available.

Throughout the rest of their studies at Columbia, David and Madison were joined at the hip, much to Lexie's chagrin. She needed Madison to take her blinders off and see what she could see.

Dating for four years throughout her studies, David was the only man she had ever known. Lexie kept on at her to play the field and open herself up to other prospects, but Madison was still extremely unsure of herself. She was convinced that David was the only man for her and, in her eyes, he could do no wrong.

Becoming like the Three Musketeers, they all applied to Johns Hopkins Hospital for their medical internship. Immediately following their initial exposure to the different fields of medicine, Madison knew that she would be bored to tears with something that didn't stimulate her mentally. The only discipline within medicine that would be acceptable was neurology.

David opted for trauma because in that field, no two days were alike, and he would really have to be on top of his game constantly.

As for Lexie ... Well, you already know that Lexie signed up for pediatrics due to her love of children. With her bubbly personality, she was able to make even the most daunting diagnosis sound like there was always an upside.

By the end of their studies, David had made up his mind to marry the girl. He just had to have her all to himself. What made Madison giddy with excitement, made Lexie sick to the pit of her stomach. How was she ever going to tell dear, sweet, soft-natured Madison that the man she was about to marry was one of the biggest flirts and cheats on campus?

When it came to Madison, David could do no wrong. In her defense, she had no one to compare him to. What did she really know about love, or how it was supposed to feel? They were comfortable enough with one another and he at least had half a brain, able to hold down a decent conversation.

When David popped the question, Madison didn't even think about it before saying yes. Little did she know, but David was exactly the type of guy who wanted to have his cake and eat it too. Within a few short months of being married, Madison began to suspect that David was cheating on her.

She'd find slips for flowers she'd never received, drinks and dinners she'd never attended, and all along, David kept both his phone and laptop password protected. The last thing that Madison wanted to believe was that David was cheating.

Whenever she'd ask him about his whereabouts, he'd be very vague in his answers, or he'd confirm that he had to work late because there were suddenly a ton of motor vehicle accidents or other emergencies.

David didn't think that Madison would really check up on him to uncover all the lies and his dirty little secrets. Things began escalating between them and the tension was rising. David's late nights turned into weekend shifts, which Madison was able to confirm that he'd arranged for other trauma surgeons to cover.

His story to them was that he and the wife needed to get away and were going to some remote, romantic destination. Madison was soon able to put two and two together to come up with four. She began checking the credit card statement whenever it arrived and could clearly see that there were patterns that had been there for a long time.

Coming to grips with the betrayal was brutal for Madison, who felt like her entire world had come to an end. "You don't get married to get divorced, Lexie! I really don't know how to dig my way out of this one."

"Why should you be the one doing the digging, Madison? You're not the guilty party here. You're actually the victim. Please don't let him get away with this any longer. He's making a complete fool out of himself and dragging you down with him. I'm so sorry that you're going through this my friend. I feel like some of this is my fault."

"How could any of this be your fault, Lexie? You're not holding a gun to his head, making him hook up with every bimbo he can find."

"You don't understand Madison. I knew that this was how David was before you guys got hitched. I should have at least told you. That's what a good friend would have done."

"Oh, my darling Lexie, always my protector—coming to the rescue for me. I can tell you that I'm not prepared to stand for it anymore. I'm a successful, accomplished surgeon and attaching the surname Webb to it is just wrong! Before I do anything about this philandering idiot, I just need to check something!" Madeline grabbed a box out of her bag and headed to the bathroom.

"You okay in there Madison?"

"I am now," cried Madison, "I am now that the home pregnancy test is negative! I would have been stuck with him if it was positive. At least this way, I can kick his ass to the curb."

It had been a long time coming and Lexie helped Madison collect boxes. Together, they boxed up as many of David's things as they could. Madison finally plucked up the courage to send him a text message.

"David, it's over. Enjoy whoever you're with, because I know everything. Please arrange to collect your stuff from the house when I'm not here. I'd appreciate you making an appointment so that Joe can let you in. I've changed all the locks, so please don't bother trying to come home. The papers will be filed as soon as I've met with my lawyers."

"Well, that's done," she said, letting out a huge sigh. "Let the battles commence!" For the first time since Madison and David walked down the aisle, Madison felt as though a massive weight had been lifted from her shoulders. "Have I done the right thing, Lexie?"

From the moment she sent the text and could see that David had read it, Madison felt a knot forming in the pit of her stomach. She cringed at the sound of her phone ringing. The caller ID showed that it was David. Lexie grabbed Madison's phone out of her hands and switched it off.

"Let him stew! He needs to know that you're serious Madison, or else he'll be all over you, making empty promises you know he's not going to keep. You are simply no longer available, by phone, or emotionally!" And so, began the lengthy divorce process that robbed Madison of six months of her life and a good part of her sanity.

Chapter 5: Huntington

"Calling Dr. Madison Watson. Dr. Watson, please contact reception." The intercom speakers buzzed with the receptionist's voice. Leaving the theatre after a grueling 18-hour procedure, she was met at the door to the theatre by her assistant, Carlie.

"Dr. Watson, there have been several messages for you from Huntington Memorial Hospital. They've asked you to please make urgent contact with them."

"Huntington Memorial?" Madison looked totally perplexed. "That's my hometown! Did they say what it was about?"

"No. Just that you needed to call Dr. Locke, from Oncology, as soon as you were available."

"Oncology? What would an oncology practitioner need me for? I'm sure they have plenty of great neurologists in California that are as good, if not better, than me!"

"They specifically asked for you and no one else. They also stressed that it was extremely urgent."

"Sure thing. I'll give Dr. Locke a call now. Just let me get out of these scrubs." Settling behind her desk, Madison dialed the familiar area code to her hometown. She'd not been back to Huntington Beach since her acceptance at Columbia. Sure, she'd kept in contact with her mother, but not even Heather Watson could convince her to return to the place that almost broke her growing up.

"Huntington Memorial. Dr. Locke here..." Madison immediately returned to the present.

"Hi Dr. Locke, this is Madison Watson from John Hopkins. I believe that you've been looking for me."

"Ah, yes, Dr. Watson! Thanks for getting back to me. Do you mind if I call you Madison? It's Patrick here. I'm the head of the oncology unit at Huntington." His voice was warm, yet matter-of-fact and Madison could tell that he was probably in his late 50's, by the tone of his voice.

"Sure, what can I do for you, Patrick?" still uncertain that Huntington Memorial had the right doctor.

"Do you perhaps remember Matthew Carmichael from Huntington Beach High School?"

"Sure, I do!" Madison exclaimed. "He's the whole reason I'm in medicine and where I am today."

"Well, the truth is that you've been requested by both Mr. Carmichael and another benefactor who would like to remain anonymous at this time to come and assist us. Mr. Carmichael has a tumor that's attached itself to his frontal lobe and, as you know, these things aren't always operable. We'd love for you to join us for a consultation to see what you think."

Madison was feeling more and more intrigued by the second. *A mysterious benefactor? How did Mr. Carmichael even know where I was? Geez, I haven't even thought about him or Huntington High School in about 15 years.* Thoughts of having to return there made the hair on the back of her neck prickle. She'd declined countless invitations from her own mother, let alone one of her old teachers.

The truth was, had it been any other teacher, Madison would have declined on the spot. But Matthew Carmichael had been the catalyst to her becoming everything she was today. He'd set the ball in motion. Who else knew about her though, who was obviously funding this whole plan, which didn't come cheaply?

"Patrick, I'm not really sure that it's such a good idea." Madison began backpedaling to worm her way out of returning to Huntington.

"Well, Madison, I must be totally honest with you. As his oncologist, things aren't looking too great for Mr. Carmichael right now. One professional to another—without considering this option, he probably doesn't have that much longer, I'm afraid. He's already showing signs of deteriorating and leaving it is only going to make things worse."

"Don't you have any neurologists there that are more suitably qualified, and obviously aware of the case?" She interrupted Patrick, still trying to get off the hook, letting him down as gently as possible.

"We do, as a matter of fact, and normally, we wouldn't even consider an out-of-house consultation, but we have heard of your reputation all the way down here, plus we believe that you're his best option. He's refusing treatment unless it's coming from you and the benefactor is standing by to transfer funds. Your trip will be fully paid for and you'd be put up for at the Hyatt for as long as you're in town."

"Well, it sounds like you've already made the arrangements for me." There was a slightly annoyed undertone in her voice. If there was one thing she simply couldn't handle, it was someone bullying her into a corner where she was no longer in control. Why was this suddenly beginning to feel like this was about to be a repeat performance of her high school years. This was one of the main reasons why she had been only too glad to see the back of Huntington.

The one thing she was sure of, Huntington had not seen this side of Madison Watson. Nobody was going to push her into a corner ever again.

"Let me try and get onto the next flight out of here and I will call you back with the details," she began telling Dr. Locke.

"That won't be necessary, Madison. There will be a driver to collect you from your apartment at 2:00 p.m. I'd pack for a couple of days if I were you, at least until Sunday evening." There was that same arrogance that Madison had grown up with her entire life, shown by all the snobs from Huntington Beach that made her school days a living hell.

"Sure... And what about all my current patients and operations here? I can't just simply up and leave?" Madison was now beginning to seethe.

"We've taken the liberty of sending our top neurologist, Dr. Burke, on a rotational exchange to handle your load while you're here. You'll find that he's a worthy ally to have in your corner." For the first time during the conversation Madison was able to relax slightly. She knew Dr. Thomas Burke well. They'd not only studied at Columbia together, but they'd also interned together at Johns Hopkins. She had heard rumors that he'd ended up at Huntington Beach. Thank goodness my patients will receive nothing but the best of care!

"Fine. How will I get around once I'm there?" Madison asked, trying to hide the frustration in her voice.

"You don't need to worry about a thing Madison. Everything has been taken care of. Once you've been collected this afternoon, you should have everything you need. I've taken the liberty of sending over a copy of Mr. Carmichael's file. I believe that you will treat it with the utmost confidence."

"Naturally." She still couldn't believe she'd just agreed to go back to Huntington.

"I'll meet you at the hospital tomorrow morning at 9:00 a.m., Dr. Watson. I'm looking forward to meeting you and having you consult on this case with me. Until then, have a safe flight, and a good evening." She heard the connection on the other side of the line go dead.

It was only then that her head started swimming with a whole lot of questions. Things like: *How do they know where I live?, Who is this benefactor who supposedly wants to remain anonymous?, What is their connection to Mr. Carmichael?, and Who decides how long I'm going to be staying in Huntington for? If I had my way, I wouldn't even be going.*

Now, now Madison, you're behaving like a bit of a spoiled brat! If it wasn't for Mr. Carmichael, you wouldn't be in the cushy position you're in right now. Surely, the least you can do is to go and do a consult? By the sounds of things from Dr. Patrick Locke, Mr. Carmichael doesn't really have too much longer to live. If that's the case, I would definitely like a chance to say goodbye. What could a couple of days in Huntington do? It's not like I'm going to run into anyone I know and besides, no one will recognize me.

I may even have a couple of hours to spend with Mother if I get the chance. I'd better get a move on if I'm going home to pack for a week. What do I even take with me? I hate these last-minute arrangements!

It was one of Madison's pet peeves, apart from liars and cheats; she simply loathed surprises and being told what to do.

***

At precisely 2:00 p.m., the front receptionist of Madison's apartment called up to let her know that there was a driver waiting for her downstairs. Madison grabbed the last of her things, including a travel pillow, as she headed out the door. She hated commercial flights and had slipped into her most comfortable pair of jeans, a sweatshirt, and ankle boots. She'd tied her hair in a high ponytail to keep it out of her face and away from her eyes. Donning her Ray Ban sunglasses to keep the glare out of her eyes, she was ready to go.

Heading downstairs, she stared at her reflection in the elevator, only to see someone closely resembling a college graduate staring back at her; not a woman in her 30s. Her choice of outfit had totally been for comfort while travelling, rather than for style.

As the elevator door opened, she was surprised to see one of the latest BMWs parked in front of her Waterfront apartment. Standing beside the passenger door was a chap with mousy-brown hair and a friendly expression on his face. Madison took him to be closer to 50 years old than to her age. Her thoughts were interrupted as he took her bags from her while opening the rear door.

"Good afternoon, Dr. Watson. My name is Steve, and I will be driving you to the airport this afternoon." Without waiting for a response, he politely closed the door, carefully packing her bags into the trunk. "We should be at the airport within about 20 minutes, given the current traffic. Is there anything you'd like to listen to on the way?"

Steve casually surveyed Dr. Watson in the rearview mirror and was wondering why it was so important that Mr. Anderson arranged for him to collect her personally. This was yet something else that Brad Anderson had never done before. If he was meeting with clients, they were usually required to make their own travel arrangements. The other thing that Steve was curious about was why he'd received explicit instructions that if she were to ask who his employer was, he was never to reveal that it was he. *Could this be the reason he was acting so funny when he was last in Baltimore?* Steve wondered with a smile on his face.

Madison took an instant liking to Steve and told him to surprise her with his music selection. Besides, she was about to be traveling in coach for the next seven to nine hours, depending on which route her ticket had been booked on. Not too surprising, the music selection came from the '80s, confirming Madison's guess that he was in his 50s, rather than 30s like she was.

Staring out the window, Madison was so lost in thought that she hardly noticed that they'd turned into a part of the airport that was reserved for private jets and aircraft. As Steve pulled up to the Gulfstream and stopped, she had to force herself to close her mouth that was hanging half open. Steve was holding the door open for her. Climbing out of the car, she suddenly felt totally underdressed. At the bottom of the stairs, someone was waiting to take her bags from Steve.

"Uh, thank, thank you Steve..." was all that Madison could mumble in Steve's general direction.

"You're most welcome, Dr. Watson. I will be here to collect you on your return to Baltimore." With that, Steve was gone.

"Welcome Dr. Watson. My name is Edward and I'm here to make your flight to Huntington as comfortable as possible. The total flying time should be about 4 hours. We should be cleared for takeoff within the next 10 minutes or so."

Once on board the Gulfstream, Madison felt like she had stepped into someone else's life completely. Not only was she totally underdressed, but she was anticipating that the Gulfstream would be filled with other passengers, not just herself.

"Feel free to sit anywhere, Dr. Watson. Can I get you something to drink in the meantime?" Edward was totally professional and had been well trained. It was clear that whoever he was working for paid him handsomely for his services. Before Madison could even ask for the medical file, he had placed it into her hands.

"This was delivered especially for you to go over. It is from Dr. Locke from Huntington Memorial."

It appears everyone knows everything about this case and I'm the last to know anything, Madison mused to herself.

"To drink, Dr. Watson?" Edward asked again.

"Um, er, what do you have?" Madison stammered, still not quite sure about this entire situation.

"We pretty much have everything, so whatever you'd like."

"In that case, I'll just have a rock shandy for now, thanks Edward. I need to go through these reports and somehow don't think that doing so under the influence would be the greatest idea. By the way, Edward, who does this jet belong to?" Madison's curiosity was getting the better of her. She simply had to ask.

Edward, on the other hand, had already been threatened with his livelihood if he ever revealed to Dr. Watson that the jet belonged to Brad Anderson. He couldn't understand it because Brad often had women companions on the jet in the early years. Although, come to think of it, he's been very quiet in the romance department for the last while. Could this petite little bombshell be the reason why?

"Your rock shandy, Dr. Watson." Edward was about to leave when Madison pressed him again for an answer.

"You can call me Madison, Edward, and you still never said who the jet belongs to."

"That's because I don't really know, uhm, Madison." Edward was clearly uncomfortable using people's first names. "It's some big corporation, as far as I know." Edward had no clue how close his guess was.

Realizing she wasn't going to get much more out of him, Madison turned her attention to the medical file in front of her. Fully engrossed in reading reports, checking scans, x-rays, and other diagnostic charts, she could tell that the prognosis for Matthew Carmichael wasn't all that great. He'd received radiation and chemotherapy, which hadn't done very much to the tumor pressing on the frontal lobe. The only possible solution would be operating, but she wasn't sure what his actual mental and physical condition was.

She would know more once she'd met with Dr. Locke in the morning, as well as then hopefully getting to meet with Matthew Carmichael himself. Placing all the medical reports and tests back in the file and envelope, Madison turned to enjoying the rock shandy.

"We'll be landing in Huntington Beach within the next 15 minutes, Dr. Watson. There will be a town car waiting to take you to the Hyatt Regency. If you go to the reception desk, they will have the keys for your suite waiting for you."

Edward repeated the instructions he'd been asked to communicate to her. Taxiing into the airstrip, sure enough, there was another car waiting for her. Driving her through Huntington, Madison was confronted by all the demons from her past. There was a distinct difference between the 'haves' and "have-nots" and she was very clearly a "have-not" geek.

She was instantly transported back some 15 or more years ago, when she wore braces on her teeth and did her best to simply fade into the background where everyone just left her alone. She'd support the school whenever she got the chance, not that she was ever noticed by anyone. For the longest time, she had the biggest crush on the captain of the football team, Bradley Anderson. Of course, he was dating the head cheerleader, Bethany Powers. They were probably married by now with lots of children.

Enough now Madison! That's why, you don't come back here; all you ever do is torture yourself over the past. When are you going to leave things where they belong? Besides, you still have Mr. tall, blonde, and dreamy eyes to think about... He didn't seem to be with anyone at the fundraiser.

When the car pulled up to the Hyatt Regency, Madison was immediately assisted with her bags, directed to the reception area, and whisked up to her suite. In all the years she'd lived in Huntington, she'd never been inside the Hyatt Regency; it was way out of her league. Now, she was finally somewhere that she could feel comfortable. She knew that even if this so-called benefactor turned out to be a dud she could still foot the bill herself.

Feeling a little too casual and not really in the mood to get all dressed up for dinner in one of the hotel's restaurants, she decided to order room service instead.

Opening the door of her suite, she could hardly hold back an audible gasp. The single suite was bigger than her entire apartment in Baltimore. It was modern and tastefully decorated, but had everything she could ever wish for.

In the center of the main table of the suite were two dozen long-stemmed red roses in a crystal vase. There was a card attached to them. Curiosity getting the better of her, she tipped the bellhop and virtually pushed him out the door. She was dying to read the card.

"Welcome home, Madison. I hope the suite is to your liking."

Urgh... It's not signed! Madison vaguely recollected the handwriting, and the heavy black ink... Could it possibly be that the mystery man and the benefactor are one and the same person? Have I been looking in the wrong place for him all along? Home? Who knows that this was my home? This is becoming a conundrum and I don't like puzzles. I'm definitely more logical than all of this.

Chapter 6: Life and Death

By 8:00 a.m., Madison was dressed professionally and ready to leave for Huntington Memorial Hospital. She'd gone over the medical charts again before going to sleep and had a nervous feeling in the pit of her stomach. She knew that if they decided to operate, that the entire procedure would be risky.

The driver was waiting for her at the entrance for the short trip to the local hospital. Madison could have managed with a hired car, seeing as this was her hometown, but the pampering was doing her a world of good. It was giving her a bit of time to unwind after what had been several pretty hectic months.

Entering Huntington Memorial, she suddenly felt nostalgic. On the odd occasion, she had been there for treatment as a child, and quite a lot had changed in the last two decades. The hospital had received a complete makeover. Still, she couldn't imagine herself ever returning to her hometown to work.

Heading for the reception desk, she was suddenly startled by the sound of a voice she recognized from the phone. "Dr. Watson?"

"That's me! I'm assuming that you're Dr. Locke?" She addressed the older gentleman whose hair was beginning to show signs of salt and pepper where it was once pitch black. He was much taller than she'd imagined, but otherwise fitted in with her initial perception perfectly.

"So, what would you like to do first?" he asked. A bit taken aback by this, Madison retorted quickly trying to be as polite as possible.

"Well, you made all the arrangements to get me here. Now that I'm here, what do you have planned?"

"Let's go and see the patient first, and that way you'll get an idea of what we're dealing with." Madison followed Patrick Locke down several corridors to the oncology wing of the hospital. Arriving at one of the more exclusive private rooms, he stopped, opened the door and motioned for her to enter.

"Madison Watson? Can that really be you?" She would have recognized the kind monotone voice of Mr. Carmichael anywhere.

"What's it been? Fifteen years or so?"

"Oh dear, Mr. Carmichael. What's a nice man like you doing in a place like this?" Madison made her very best attempt at adding a little humor to what was very obviously a serious situation. Staring back at her was a former shadow of her physics teacher who, just a few years before, had been so full of life and vitality. The radiation and chemotherapy had clearly taken their toll on his systems and he'd lost a lot of weight. His color was also not looking as good as Madison had hoped.

"Well, you called for me, and how could I say no to my favorite teacher of all time?" She was trying to sound as reassuring as she could. She now understood the sense of urgency that Dr. Locke had tried to communicate with her over the phone not even 24 hours before. "Mr. C., Dr. Locke and I are just going to meet quickly, and I want to have a look at some of your records. I promise that I'll be back before you know it."

Dr. Locke was clearly impressed with her bedside manner and realized that she'd already made her assessment of his patient. Leaving the room, he was anxious to hear what the top neurosurgeon from Johns Hopkins had to say about him.

Several corridors away, they were standing in his office where he had access to all the latest equipment.

Now we're talking! At least I'll be able to see the scans more clearly than relying on the bad lighting in the jet. Madison wasted no time in getting straight to the point.

"Well, Patrick, I'm not sure what you want me to tell you that Thomas Burke wouldn't have already said. That tumor is probably going to kill him. I was hoping that he was going to look better than he does. I'm not even sure whether he'll survive the operation, if we are successful."

"What are you trying to tell me Madison? I know that he's not looking all that great because he's coming off the back of 20 or so chemo treatments in an effort to shrink this monster tumor!"

"And? Has any of it worked as yet?" She darts her eyes over to the large computer screens where, for the first time, she's able to really see what she's dealing with.

"Yes, and no." Patrick answers. "Initially, it was bigger, and it began responding well to the chemo regimen we had him on and then, all of a sudden, it stopped."

"That's typical of a tumor located where it is..." Madison stared off into the distance, as she was trying to work through each of the steps of an intricate operation in her mind, which was something she did before every major surgery. This is what had put her at the top of her game. She seldom took risks unless they were calculated ones, which is why she had such a high recovery ratio and was so well sought after as a neurosurgeon.

"Patrick, I must tell you that I'm not willing to do his procedure. I think that it's very risky and could potentially kill him on the table."

"What do you want me to tell him, Madison? You were specifically requested by both him and..." Patrick stopped mid-sentence, realizing that he was about to disclose who the private benefactor was.

"Him and whom? Madison queried.

"I was going to say his benefactor," Patrick responded, hoping to avoid further questions about his almost blunder.

"Yeah, and who might this benefactor be? I notice that he's booked one of the most expensive suites, I get flown out here on a private jet, and put up at the Hyatt Regency for a week. This is definitely not someone who is in Matthew Carmichael's social circles! I need to know who I'm working for. Mr. Carmichael, or someone else?" She realized her voice was beginning to rise above its normal tone.

"I'm sorry, but they've insisted on remaining anonymous. I will reach out and ask whether I can disclose who they are, seeing as you insist, but I'm not sure that will do any good."

"Well, you do that. In the meantime, I'm going back to sit with Matthew for a while. I have some 15 years' worth of catching up to do and I need to analyze whether mentally he will handle this brutal operation." With that, she turned on her heels and headed back to Matthew's room. Gently knocking on the door, she entered the room and, finding Matthew with his eyes closed, was about to leave.

"Madison, wait! Don't go just yet!" Matthew motioned for her to come and take a seat next to him. Offering his hand, he took her dainty hand in his. "You probably think that I'm just a silly old man requesting a consultation from you."

"Not at all, Mr. C. As a matter of fact, I feel rather honored by it. I mean, that after all these years, you even remember me."

"Remember you? How could I ever forget one of the brightest students I had in my physics class? I've been following your career for years young lady! Even your big, fancy dinner a few months ago where you raised all that money for your research."

Madison felt the color begin to rise in her cheeks as she remembered the blonde, blue-eyed mystery man that she'd not been able to find yet. She was flustered that even now, the thought of him still had an intense influence on her emotions.

"Madison, there's nobody else that I would trust with this tumor, other than you. I value your medical expertise and I know that there's no way you're likely to bullshit me with some or other medical speak."

It's rather amusing to hear Matthew Carmichael swear! He was always so stiff upper lip and well-bred of class. Then again, I guess that was then and this is now. Being on death's door will probably do that to you.

"Well, I promise that I'll try to not do any of those things to you Matthew. I'll be very honest though; it's not looking very good. I'd like you to think long and hard about what you want." Madison was quite serious. "I would have preferred for you to be healthier before facing this operation. If you survive it, and that's a big if, then the road to recovery is going to be a long one. Do you have someone who you can rely on to take good care of you?"

"I guess that I do, come to think of it…" Matthew also stopped short.

Why do I get the feeling that everyone is trying to hide something from me?

"I'll tell you what Matthew, if you show sufficient recovery over the next few days while I'm still here and you insist on having this operation done, then I'll do it for you. As it stands now though, I'm not all that happy about it." With that, she gave him a gentle kiss on the forehead and left to find Patrick.

***

True to her word, Madison stayed for several days visiting with Matthew daily to lift his spirits and confirm whether he would be able to survive the procedure if she decided to take the risk. Risk was really the operative word. By day 3, Matthew was beginning to show some signs of improvement and Madison was hoping beyond all hope that he was turning the corner to recovery.

Consulting with Patrick again, she began investigating a surgical team that were well versed with the procedure she needed to perform. Back home, she didn't even need to think about her team, as they'd all been working together for years and every one of them could easily manage fairly challenging surgeries. They'd been under her guidance for long enough.

Madison didn't feel the same level of confidence at Huntington. Insisting on meeting with each team member, or potential team member, was something she hadn't had to do for a number of years. Yet, she wasn't feeling confident working with staff who weren't her own, even if they'd been hand-picked by Thomas Burke. Admittedly, Thomas and

Madison had a similar style of working, but that had been more than a decade ago and a lot could change in that time.

Feeling the sudden urge to speak with her old colleague, she dialed through to John Hopkins' switchboard and asked for him.

"Dr. Burke here," answered Thomas.

"Hey Tom. It's Madison. How's it going with everything there?" Suddenly feeling a bit homesick, it was the first thing that came to mind.

"Tell me why you didn't want to touch the Carmichael case. I've heard some rumors."

"Hey there Madison. I can't say that I'm surprised to be hearing from you. I didn't want to touch the case because you and I both know what the odds are of the surgery being successful. Odds are odds, and I don't like playing them when they're not in my favor."

"What about your team, Tom? Are they capable of working under me and taking direction with this kind of pressure?"

"Sure, I guess so..."

"I'm going to need more than an 'I guess so.' I'm going to need confirmation that none of them are going to crack on me in the theatre. You know that this could potentially be a long one, and it's going to be tricky."

"All that I can say, Madison, is that they've been trained exactly the same way as we were."

"Thanks Tom. That's all that I really need to know for now."

***

"Okay Patrick, let's give it a go! I'm going to speak with Matthew one last time to see where he's head is at. If he's still on board, then let's book an operating room for Thursday night."

"Sure Madison. Let me know what he says, and I'll make all the arrangements."

"Matthew, it's me. I'm back again! I've come to ask you one last time what you want to do with this thing in your head."

"Oh Madison, I've lived a great life. I don't want to have to go through the rest of my days wasting away like this. They've already told me what's likely to happen if it manages to lodge itself further into my frontal lobe. I don't think that I want to live like that either."

"Matthew, there's a big difference between thinking that you don't want to live like that and not living like that. You have to understand all the risks here and the fact that you may very well not make it, or there may be frontal lobe damage when we remove it. Unfortunately, I won't know until I get in there."

"Madison, I want the surgery, please. You're the best, and I'm ready to take my chances. Whatever is meant to happen will happen!"

***

Fourteen hours into the operation and Madison was not only exhausted, but she was also as frustrated as hell. It's one thing operating on a total stranger, but it's totally different operating on someone she knew extremely well—someone who molded her and shaped her, basically giving her the life she has.

The tumor was exactly as she suspected, well entrenched into the frontal lobe with its demonic tentacles finding their way right into Matthew's brain. Even Madison, with her tiny fingers and fine method of working, was battling to sever each of the seemingly countless cells from the tumor in an attempt to remove it.

There had also been several times during the last few hours where Matthew's heart had arrested, and they had to bring him back. Madison wasn't sure how much more his heart would be able to withstand with the pounding it was getting. Closely monitoring his vitals, she tried time and time again to go back in and remove the tumor piece by piece, without damaging his brain in the process.

Once again, Matthew flatlined and Madison's heart sank.

"Come on Matthew, come on Matthew, you can do this, you know you can," she whispered in his ear. The nursing staff were back with the paddles, trying to revive him. This time, it seemed to be taking longer. Madison's heart was beginning to climb into her throat. There was just no way she was going to be the cause of this man's death on the operating table. "COME ON MATTHEW!" she screamed, much to the surprise of the rest of the nursing team. They knew that she had a vested interest in this case, but how vested, they didn't know.

Matthew's heart had refused to restart after about ten attempts using the defibrillating equipment. One of the theatre staff mentioned to Madison that she needed to call the time of death. In a complete daze, Madison nodded in her general direction and looked at the clock on the wall.

"Time of death 05:45."

Madison felt as though she was going to throw up. She knew there had been a huge risk involved, and she knew what Matthew's wishes had been. He was one of the first patients she'd lost on a table in a while. What made this worse was that he was a friend. She wasn't able to convince him not to have the operation. Madison felt gutted.

***

The least I can do is to stay in town for the funeral. Is there even going to be a funeral?

Still feeling sorry for herself, she wasn't sure how all of this was going to impact her being in Huntington.

How would all of this play out with the benefactor? They were obviously paying for me to save his life. Now what?

Madison didn't have much longer to wait for her answer. Arriving back at her suite, feeling battered and bruised, she was handed a note by the receptionist. Inside, it contained vouchers for her to visit the beauty spa for the day. She was of the mind to hand the vouchers back, but decided that a massage may be just what she needed to clear her head.

Back in her suite, there were another two dozen long-stemmed roses, with another note that read, *"I'm so sorry. I know you tried your best!"*

Who keeps on sending these notes? How are they totally in the loop with everything that is going on?

What Madison had failed to see throughout the operation was the tall figure at the back of the observation booth. He felt her frustration and emotional pain as they were unable to revive Matthew Carmichael for a final time.

All the funeral arrangements would be taken care of by Brad. He would personally pick out the best casket that money could buy and pay for him to have a resting place worthy of a man of his stature.

The local paper ran a half-page tribute to the teacher who had touched so many lives at Huntington Bay High School. It confirmed that the funeral would take place on the following Monday at a local upmarket funeral home.

While relaxing having her spa treatments, Madison decided to update Lexie on everything that had happened. Lexie was probably one of the few people who knew that it was Matthew Carmichael who had been a contributing factor to her success. Lexie was still very curious about who kept sending her these gifts, and the jet, and the private room, and, and, and... she kept pressing Madison for answers and all the while, Madison was no closer to the truth herself.

Madison was deep in thought about what had transpired over the last few hours. She'd hardly managed to sleep, replaying every step of the medical procedure over and over again in her head. She was ruminating about whether things may have turned out differently if she was with her own team back at Johns Hopkins. There were too many questions without answers.

While having her hair styled, after her massage and facial, she realized she had nothing suitable to wear to the funeral on Monday. She'd have to go shopping, and she knew she was bound to run into someone from high school. At this stage, she simply had no energy to go anywhere or do anything.

Feeling relaxed and somewhat rejuvenated, she returned to her room only to find several gift boxes, each one with a lavish bow on it, on her bed. The note read, *"I'm sure you never planned for this."*

Each of the largest boxes contained an exquisite black outfit, in her exact size. Other boxes contained shoes of different heights, but also in her correct size. And finally, there were two tasteful black hats with small black veils that she could wear to complete whichever of the outfits she chose to wear. She decided that these must be on consignment and rang down to the reception desk to check.

"No, Dr. Watson. Each of those garments has been specifically chosen for you and the instructions are that you are to keep all of them." Madison was shocked, but felt like a little child! Trying every outfit on, she realized why they'd all been given to her. Some of them were definitely not what you'd call funeral material. Instead, they verged more on risqué little black numbers! Included with the shoes were Jimmy Choo heels. Now, how would someone know that those were her all-time favorite shoes?

She began to feel that there were either cameras in her room, or someone knew more about her than she knew herself. Whoever these gifts were coming from, the individual had some pretty expensive taste. One of the last gifts she opened was a large bottle of Joy Baccarat perfume. This was the type of perfume that she could only dream of affording, even on her current salary. This was a luxury she simply couldn't afford.

Settling on an outfit for the funeral, Madison had chosen a tasteful little black number that accentuated her tiny figure, but was still modest enough to honor her dear friend. In case there was anyone there from her high school year, she'd be able to hide at least half of her face away behind a veil, while having all her hair away from her face.

Chapter 7: Unmasked

Funerals are always somber affairs and for Madison, this one was no exception. It was probably made worse by the fact that she actually was holding Matthew Carmichael's brain in her hands when he died.

Why did I ever agree to operate on him? I knew the risks. Probably better than anyone... Why did I let Matthew convince me to go ahead anyway? Yes, he may have experienced further discomfort if Patrick decided to give him more chemo. At least he might have still had a couple of months to say his goodbyes.

Hundreds of thoughts seemed to attack Madison all at once from different angles while she got ready for the funeral. Drawing her hair up behind her head in an upward swirl, she could adjust the small black hat she'd chosen to wear with one of the simple black dresses and medium-height plain, black shoes. Black was certainly her color as it made her emerald eyes sparkle even more—the sparkle today was the result of many tears shed over the last few days.

Madison added some light color to her cheeks after she'd used a ton of foundation to cover the dark rings under her eyes gained from hardly sleeping since the surgery. She rounded off her makeup with a very light touch of powder to get rid of the shine and an almost neutral shade of lipstick. The last thing she wanted to look like was one of the typical plastic bimbos she was sure would make an appearance at the funeral home.

Could they just get this funeral thing over with so she could return to her normal life in Baltimore? She was missing her own apartment, her own things, and especially at a time like this, she could really do with some "Lexie downtime."

When the two of them each had an especially bad day at the hospital, they'd either find a quiet bar to drown their sorrows with a pitcher of Sangria, or they'd settle for a couple of tubs of Rocky Road, two spoons, and a soppy chick-flick movie on Netflix while laying on Madison's bed.

Once again, Jerome, the Huntington driver, was waiting for her downstairs. Madison greeted him warmly and then once again retracted into her shell as she stared out the window at some familiar, yet modernized, cityscapes around her. She was totally lost in thought when they arrived at the funeral home.

As anticipated, quite a large crowd had already gathered and were making their way to the private, intimate, funeral home's chapel. Thankfully, nobody seemed to have recognized her, although she was getting some stares from many of the faces that she remembered from high school. It felt as though it were just yesterday that they were tormenting her in the hallways.

Sitting toward the middle of the chapel, Madison thought that she recognized the back of a well-maintained blonde head sitting in one of the front rows. It was not just the back of the head she recognized, but the same athletic build, and the black suit he was wearing was definitely not off the rack.

Her attention was now piqued with interest, and she desperately wanted him to turn sideways, or even around so she could get an idea of who he was. Questions began swirling around in her head, making her feel dizzy. She was definitely feeling weak in the knees.

Stop it Madison! You're being an idiot. How could that possibly be the same man? That was Baltimore. You're now sitting in a funeral parlor in Huntington Beach at the funeral of one of your former school teachers. Two and two just don't add up. You're so besotted with this man that you'd see him anywhere.

As if he could hear her thoughts, Brad unexpectedly turned around and once again, their eyes became fixed upon one another. From the moment she saw him, she knew exactly who he was.

What the hell? What is Brad Anderson doing here? Better still, could it actually have been Brad Anderson in Baltimore? Could he have been the benefactor behind Matthew Carmichael's treatment? If so, how? How could he afford to pay for all of this? How did he even know Matthew Carmichael?

He was a jock in high school, and his kind weren't exactly known for being any good at anything other than picking up cheerleaders and making touchdowns. Speaking of which, where was Bethany? Madison realized that Brad seemed to be there on his own.

How can he afford to be wearing a suit like that? Brad Anderson? Was he behind all those gifts?

Suddenly, Madison could feel the color in her cheeks begin to flush bright crimson.

Oh, I hope that my foundation and powder keep this covered and to myself. How could he possibly know my size, my favorite shoes, and everything else about me?

Did he know that for all the years we were in high school together, I had the biggest crush on him? Seems like nothing has changed, other than the way he looks right now! Oh crap, why is he still staring at me that way? It's the same as in Baltimore. I can't keep looking at him! Those icy blue eyes are finding their way deep into my soul.

Brad gave her a quick nod and flashed her a typical Anderson smile; one that she knew so well, but hadn't seen in about 15 years or so. Whatever had happened to him, it seemed as though he had been favored by fortune. Not surprising though, as he had been voted as most likely to succeed in anything he put his mind to.

Not sure whether she wanted to find out or not, Madison sank a bit lower into her seat, breaking his gaze. Now, she just felt like the silly little schoolgirl she'd put behind her at the moment she stepped into her dorm at Columbia, with the help of Lexie, of course.

She resolved to sit upright and at least pay Matthew Carmichael the respect he was due. The eulogy was befitting of such a wonderful teacher. Madison was beginning to put two and two together again. Brad had probably inherited the family fortune, seeing as they always appeared to be financially stable. This is probably old Huntington Beach money!

As the memorial service was coming to an end, Madison felt her heart beginning to find its way into her throat. Knowing that this was an anatomical anomaly, she tried to regain her composure, realizing that she'd have to go over and finally strike up a conversation with her high school crush—something she'd only dreamed about for five years throughout high school, yet never quite plucking up the courage to do so.

Before she could get the thought out of her mind, he was suddenly next to her.

"Dr. Madison Watson, from Baltimore! My name is…"

"Brad Anderson!" Madison interrupted.

"Er, umm… How did you know that?" Brad seemed flustered that she knew who he was.

He really doesn't know who I am, does he? Madison was feeling as though she had one up on the situation for a change, seeing as he'd been calling the shots for the last week. He'd been like a puppet-master, pulling all the strings from the outside, while all the while, Madison would never have guessed it was him.

"I know more about you than you realize, Brad!" she retorted, clearly feeling a little amused by the cat and mouse game they were playing.

How could she though? I'd given explicit instructions to everyone to leave my name out of it, until this morning. I'm still certain that she had no idea that I had anything to do with any of this. Brad was uncharacteristically confused.

"How do you know who I am?"

"I can say the same about you, but then again, you were at my fundraising event in Baltimore. From there, it's pretty easy to pick up the breadcrumbs by following the media hype. What happened to you? I was about to come and say thank you for your very generous donation and you disappeared on me."

"I er… needed to get back to the office for a very important conference call. I'll tell you what, meet me for cocktails tonight in the Red Chair Lounge at 7:00 p.m. and we can compare notes then. You can share your story and I'll maybe let you in on mine."

There was that same cocky, arrogant, style of communication that Madison knew only too well from Huntington Beach High School. This time, she wasn't likely to be bullied though. She had more than enough experience under her belt and would easily make very short work of Brad Anderson if he thought he was going to get the better of her.

"I'll meet you tonight, on one condition," she found herself saying to the piercing blue eyes that she'd been all gaga for since she was a teenager.

"You name it." Brad said with a hint of intrigue.

"This will be a 'no holds barred' frank conversation." You need to be prepared to tell me everything."

"Well, I will tell you what I can. Understand that there are some things that a business professional has to keep secret. Call it the same as a doctor-patient confidentiality clause."

"Sure, I can live with that!"

Her sparkling emerald eyes darted back and forth trying desperately to sum up the enigma standing in front of her. Finally, some of the pieces of the puzzle were beginning to fall into place.

How did he manage to find me though and knowing what I looked back in high school, why is he even giving me the time of day right now? I'm sure that he has more than enough women chasing after him to be worried about me.

Placing some of the long-stemmed red roses that she'd brought along from the hotel on Matthew's grave, she suddenly felt a hand on her elbow to steady her.

"I see you got the flowers," Brad whispered in her ear. "At least you're putting them to good use. Old Matthew would have really appreciated this."

"Old Matthew?" Who the hell did Brad think he was? How could he possibly even know what Matthew was like? In his final days at the hospital, she didn't recall seeing Brad there once. How could he just waltz in here as if he owned the place?

Madison was beginning to regret her decision to accept Brad's invitation for drinks. Chances are, she was going to end up saying things she knew she'd regret later. She was overwhelmed with memories of a much younger version of the man who stood before her today. Admittedly, he had definitely become more attractive with age.

The question was whether his personality was still the same, or whether it matched the gorgeous man who was suggesting drinks to "compare notes."

Walking back to where Jerome was waiting for her, she could feel those ice-blue eyes taking in every inch of her body and she wasn't quite sure whether she should feel excited about it, or whether she should head for the hills. How could she get hold of him to cancel drinks? She began trying to reason with herself why it wasn't such a great idea after all. What would they talk about? Their years at school? The jock and the geek story never quite has a happy ending.

Arriving back at the hotel, Madison could feel the sweltering heat of the midday summer sun beating down on her, especially wearing all black for the funeral. From her suite, the hotel pool looked cool and inviting. Realizing that she hadn't packed anything remotely suitable for relaxing, other than the jeans she'd arrived in, Madison decided to phone the concierge.

While waiting for the concierge to get back to her, Madison decided to do a little digging of her own. Now that she knew that Brad Anderson was possibly behind everything, she couldn't wait to find out more about him. Opening her laptop, she began typing "Bradley Anderson" into the Google search engine. To her surprise, within a matter of seconds, there were several hundred thousand hits that she could scroll through to learn more about him. Adding her tablet to her bag, this would definitely require an afternoon of serious investigation down at the pool!

Within half an hour, there was a knock at the door by the concierge who presented her with a large variety of swimwear in her size, sunblock, and even a sarong she could wear over her swimsuit. Choosing a classic bikini and a one-piece costume that accentuated all the right places, leaving little to the imagination, Madison was determined to get some sun before heading home to Baltimore.

Donning the floral bikini, with the sarong tied around her waist, sunblock, a good book in her bag, and her tablet, she completed the ensemble with a wide-brimmed hat to hide her hair and her UV protective Ray Bans. Taking the private elevator down to the pool deck, she found a lounge chair sitting in sufficient sun that was close to the water. She could hardly recall the last time she'd been in the sun. Her creamy complexion gave it away though.

Settling down on the lounger, she decided to call Lexie to update her with all the latest in the Benefactor Brad saga. Not only was she able to update Lexie, but she could confirm that he was actually her "mystery man" from the Baltimore Art Museum; the one who had donated the $2,000,000. And somehow, he seemed to be connected to her whole reason for being in Huntington in the first place.

Lexie just let out one of her really loud laughs, one that only Lexie could pull off (maybe because of her Italian side). "And here you go all the way across the country to find that the man of your dreams is actually just the boy next door! He's been under your nose all this time, Madison!"

"But that's the thing Lexie, I don't think that he really knows who I am! Yes, he knows me as Dr. Madison Watson, but he's not putting two and two together and coming up with the Maddie Watson that was at school with him, or a year below him while at Huntington High. If he did, I think he'd be running a mile, in the opposite direction."

Putting the phone down, Madison began doing her research, only to discover how and why Brad Anderson could afford all the fancy things in life—the jet, the luxury suite at the hotel, the clothes, the roses, and even bringing her back to Huntington to operate on Matthew. Hell, he could have easily added a few more zeros onto the check in Baltimore without even flinching.

I'm not really sure how I feel about all this additional information. Does it make him more of a prospect or merely like a huge red flag to a bull? I'm sure that he must view anyone trying to get into his pants as a gold-digger. Madison blushed bright red at the thought of getting into his pants, and decided it was time to cool off in the pool.

Several hours in the sun and pool along with some cocktails were beginning to make Madison giddy. Was it that, or the thought that in the next two hours she would be sitting directly across from the man who was literally the boy of her dreams in high school? *What to wear?* she thought to herself. *And this time it will not be an outfit paid for by Brad Anderson.*

Once again, the concierge came to the rescue with several outfits from some of the exclusive boutiques in the hotel. Madison had to admit to herself that she felt like a little girl in a candy store with such a selection of exquisite outfits. This time though, she would pay for it herself. She certainly didn't need Brad's charity any longer.

Choosing a lace burgundy figure-hugging dress with a low plunging neckline and sheer lace long sleeves, all that Madison needed was to complete the outfit with something special. She decided to leave her hair down for once, her long raven curls running half-way down the back of the dress that was opened to her tiny waist.

Opting for the black stilettos that Brad had bought her, she searched through her things to find a set of diamante earrings and matching necklace. The necklace sat directly above her cleavage. This evening called for a bit more color to her lips to match the outfit, as well as some heavier shadow on her eyes, making them extra smoky. Spraying a dash of the Joy Baccarat, she surveyed her handiwork before grabbing her clutch bag and heading on out the door.

Waiting for her at the door to the cocktail lounge stood Brad, looking drop-dead gorgeous. He was wearing a charcoal three-piece suit that once again looked as though he'd been poured into it, body-hugging slim fit pants, and an open-necked white shirt. In his hands, he held a single, long-stemmed red rose.

"You look gorgeous as ever Madison," Brad greeted, although he was clearly taken aback that she was not wearing one of the outfits he'd sent to her. "Shall we go in?"

Feeling weak at the knees—and it wasn't from the height of the Jimmy Choo heels—all that Madison could manage was a nod. What was it about this man that held her so captivated, even after all these years?

Chapter 8: Falling For You

Brad hoped that Madison wouldn't notice how totally nervous he was. Yes, he came across as being totally assertive whenever he was in a boardroom filled with high-level business executives, but one look from those almond-shaped emerald eyes, and he could get lost in them forever. He was desperately trying to hide the instant effect she was having on him.

Trying his best to be in control of the situation, he felt like a silly little schoolboy, although he had no reason for feeling that way. She looked like a million dollars in a deep wine-colored dress with enough lace on it that he could only imagine being able to sink his teeth into. The plunging neckline revealed her firm breasts which he was struggling to take his eyes off of.

Stopping just below her thighs, he could just use his imagination regarding what was higher, but he dare not even go there right now, not before their first drink. Trying to clear his throat, he was unexpectedly pleased that he'd dispensed with the more formal tie and decided to leave his top button undone.

Touching the small of her back ever so gently, he motioned for them to sit in a quiet corner where there were comfortable chairs and a table especially made for cocktails or drinks. Madison almost moaned out loud as his fingers brushed her bare skin. His touch was electrifying. One thing for sure, there was definitely chemistry between them.

She realized that she hadn't imagined his gaze undressing her in Baltimore, and he'd pretty much done something similar, but a whole lot quicker, once she arrived this evening. Although she wasn't going to complain about it too much, she'd been having some pretty provocative thoughts of her own, seeing him away from the morbid setting of the cemetery.

Was there was any truth to the rumor that funerals made people want to have sex?

Returning to reality, she realized they were no longer alone, as a server had joined them, and Brad was ordering one of their finest bottles of Dom Perignon.

Whatever are we going to talk about, there is no way I can let on that I am Maddie Watson, geek girl extraordinaire from Huntington High some 15 years ago. That would just be plain awkward, seeing as he hadn't mentioned it. I'm totally convinced that he has no idea.

The server was like an absolute godsend, appearing just at the right moment with the most exquisite champagne flutes Madison had ever seen, the bottle of Dom, which they opened then and there, pouring just the right amount into each glass, and setting the rest of the bottle into a wine cooler beside Brad.

"Well, Dr. Madison Watson, here's to you!" Brad was raising his glass in a toast to her health. It was the way that he said it that made Madison feel a little uneasy.

"Can we please start over?" Madison heard herself responding to Brad out loud. "Please could we dispense with all the formalities, and the titles? Just call me Madison." To be honest, it was a pet peeve of Madison's to constantly have her title attached to her name. That was something that David had always insisted on doing and it would drive Madison insane.

"Sure, I can live with that," Brad answered. They clinked their glasses together which sounded like a symphony as they were crystal. There was something to be said for drinking champagne out of crystal glasses rather than conventional glasses. It even tasted classier. "So," Brad began, "you mentioned that you wanted a 'no holds barred' frank conversation this evening. Let me have it. I promise to be as upfront and honest as I can be."

At the same time, his stomach was completely in knots. *What could she possibly have unearthed about me that she would make such a statement at the cemetery?*

"How did you manage to get into Princeton?" was the first question that blurted out of Madison's mouth, immediately wishing she could take it back because she realized it could put her right in the firing line.

"That's quite a long story actually, but I guess you're not going anywhere right now, so I may as well tell you. You probably guessed that I went to Huntington High School. I was a typical jock and didn't pay too much attention to my grades until the last two years of school. It was thanks to Matthew Carmichael that I was able to change my attitude. He would tutor me after football practice and at nighttime in his own home. When it came down to getting into college, he was the one who convinced me to apply to Princeton. He even wrote a glowing letter of recommendation. So, although I got into Princeton on a full-ride football scholarship, along with being accepted for Business Management, the rest, as they say, is history."

"How did you know I went to Princeton in any event?" Brad was intrigued.

"It's amazing what a little surfing on the internet can get you," she smiled warmly.

Brad's heart was busy melting further and further into the bottom of his shoes. He had no idea why this clearly intelligent, utterly gorgeous woman was sitting with him sharing a bottle of Dom Perignon. Although he had dated hundreds of women before, none of them were quite as intriguing and intellectually stimulating as Madison Watson.

"And what about you? I must admit that there's very little about you available on the internet before Columbia University. It appears like you only materialized there. What's your story?" By this time, Brad was almost sitting on the edge of his seat, leaning in toward her.

"Well, quite like your own really. Small-town girl, dreams of getting the hell out of Dodge. Thanks to a teacher who also happened to take an interest in me insisting that I apply to a whole lot of colleges. For me, Columbia was my first choice for studying medicine and then an internship at Johns Hopkins, and I've been there ever since."

"Why is such a gorgeous woman not married with a house full of kids?" If the truth be told, Brad knew all about David Webb and the messy divorce that Madison had been through. He was testing her to see whether she felt comfortable enough to be able to share the truth with him.

"I actually was married for about four years. Let's just say that it didn't end very well/ I'm still trying to pick up the pieces and it's been a bit of a rough year for me. Can we just leave it at that? I don't want to waste such a glorious evening speaking about my ex." Madison was surprised by how comfortable she felt sharing this information with him.

Was it the champagne or the company? Madison was suddenly feeling very warm and fuzzy and wonderfully comfortable with Brad. The Dom Perignon was making her feel lightheaded and giddy at the same time. She imagined how comfortable it would be snuggling into his arms.

"What would you like to eat Madison?" Brad caught her mid thought.

"Surprise me Brad. I know this is your stomping ground and you probably know all the coolest places in town."

"How could you possibly know that?" Brad hardly ever came back to Huntington Beach, as a matter of fact, he was a lot like Madison in that respect. Watching the City Limits Exit sign to Huntington Bay in his rearview mirror had been one of the highlights of his high school year. Heading off to Princeton changed an egotistical jock into the man of principles that was sitting in front of the girl of his dreams.

"I'll tell you what. You choose the type of food you'd like to eat, and I'll make arrangements for tomorrow."

"Tomorrow?" Madison looked at him with her smoky eyes.

Those long lashes were simply too long and gorgeous to be natural.

Batting her eyes at him, she had no idea what she was doing to him physically. He wanted her so badly, but that would be in poor taste, plus he had specific rules when it came to dating.

Dating? Could this be the start of something real?

Brad knew what he was feeling, and by the looks of things, Madison was feeling the same way, but he really wasn't sure. With all his business experience and meeting executives, summing them up in seconds was easy. In many ways, she was one of the most difficult people for him to read.

"Let's just do some conventional cuisine this evening. After the funeral today, I'm really not in the mood to even think about restaurants." Madison knew that she had to get some food into her before she made a complete fool of herself with Brad. "Is there perhaps a restaurant close by?"

"Yes, as a matter of fact, there's a really good one that's just around the corner. I will get them to send over our bottle of champagne," he said motioning for the server who was standing like a soldier at attention just out of earshot.

Meanwhile, Madison excused herself to powder her nose. Staring back at her reflection in the bathroom mirror, Madison fixed some of the mascara that was sticking some of her long lashes together. Reapplying another layer of dark lipstick, she repositioned her breasts to reveal a bit more cleavage. Trying to pull the bottom of the dress down a little further than it was, she realized that her cheeks were looking rather flushed. Unable to tell whether it was the champagne or the man, Madison drew a large breath, pulled her shoulders back, and resolved that she wasn't going to make this conquest an easy one for the gorgeous Mr. Anderson.

By the time she was done, Brad was once again standing by to guide her to their table, following the Maître d' to a quiet corner table overlooking the sea. Madison's temptation to look at her watch was interrupted by another server with menus and their glasses of champagne from the lounge. Leaning forward, Madison could feel Brad staring at her breasts as he asked whether he could order for both of them.

She found herself agreeing with him. Who could ever say no to those blue eyes? As much as he seemed to be devouring her with his eyes, she was every bit as aroused by his muscular physique. He'd removed his jacket to reveal arms that were extremely well defined. She could immediately tell that he was extremely fit and worked out regularly. The front of his shirt revealed some fine, blonde chest hairs on sun-kissed skin.

Madison licked her lips and bit her bottom lip rather provocatively, imagining him without his shirt on. Not missing a beat, Brad noticed the tiny provocative gesture and imagined what those cherry lips would taste like, especially mixed with champagne. Catching himself, Brad sat back up. He was becoming far too mesmerized by this enchantress on their first evening out.

He had an extremely strict, no-fooling-around-on-a-first-date policy. This cut through a lot of the nonsense and all the little gold-diggers that had found him online. He'd had more than his fair share of those. But Madison was different. She was a strong, independent woman who very clearly knew what she wanted out of life. *How am I ever going to convince her to stay in California for a while longer?* Now that Matthew was dead, there really was no reason for her to stay and she will probably want to head straight back to Baltimore.

All throughout dinner, they kept up the small talk. Madison was feeling rather sad about having to go back to Baltimore. She wanted to spend some more time getting to know the man sitting opposite her. He was not the spoiled young schoolboy she'd fallen for all those years ago at Huntington Beach High School. Now, he was plain Mr. hot, hot, hot, and the longer she thought about it, the more she realized he was driving her crazy. Call it lust, desire, whatever... she wanted whatever he was offering.

Finally reaching for one of her hands, he clasped her dainty fingers between both of his and asked the question they'd both been trying to avoid the whole night,

"When do you need the jet to take you back, Madison?" His face became more serious than she'd seen the whole evening.

"Are you trying to get rid of me this quickly?" she quipped with a broad smile.

"On the contrary," Brad answered sincerely. "I'll tell you what. Why don't you pack your bags tonight and I'll fetch you first thing in the morning. Come and spend a few days with me and when you're ready to get back, I'll have the jet standing by to take you home." Brad was taking a total stab in the dark that she was experiencing the same emotions as he was and wasn't quite ready to let them go just yet.

He was absolutely spot on, but Madison came back with a response which he wasn't expecting at all.

"Brad, I'd really love to take you up on your offer, which I'm sure has worked on a lot of women before me, but I have a serious job I need to get back to in Baltimore. Unfortunately, I don't have the luxury of being able to take off whenever I want."

"I'm mortally wounded Madison," he said, both hands over his heart. "How could you ever assume such a thing about me?"

"Well, your online profile for one thing shows you with a different piece of arm candy in each photograph taken, other than your professional business pictures."

She was right about the bevy of beauties that had been part of Brad's past, but it was exactly that, in the past. However, Madison was going to need a whole lot more convincing. There was something comfortable and familiar about her.

Although she was enjoying the time with Brad, Madison could tell she'd had enough to drink and wasn't sure she'd be able to control herself around Brad for much longer if she stayed.

"Brad, I've really had the most magical evening with you tonight. The champagne has been great, the food and company have all been excellent, but I really need to say goodnight."

"Please reconsider my offer Madison, even if it's just for a day or so." Brad was a master negotiator. When he could sense victory, he wasn't one to back down. For him, Madison would have been the ultimate prize right now. He needed to pull in some favors and quickly if he wasn't to lose his chance with her again.

Always the consummate gentleman, he walked her to the elevator that would take her away from him for a few hours. Unable to resist the urge he'd had the whole night, he wrapped one arm around the small of her back, drawing her close to him, and bending down towards her cherry-red lips. He kissed her gently, and then withdrew, staring intently into her bright green eyes until the elevator arrived.

Kissing her on the back of her hand, he turned and disappeared into the dark of the night, as the elevator doors closed. Madison could hear her own heart beating inside her chest and leaned against the back of the elevator all the way up to her suite. Once inside, she removed her shoes at the door and jumped on the king size bed face-down to muffle her frustrated screams. Why does she have to go back to Baltimore, just when things with Brad are starting to heat up?

Glancing at the clock, she reached for her mobile to call Lexie. Just as she was about to press the speed dial for Lexie, in came a text from Brad.

"Sweetest of dreams, darling Madison. 'Til tomorrow, Brad"

Oh my word, this man is relentless!

"Lexie, I have had one of the best evenings ever! He wants me to stay and go away with him!"

"So sister, whatever are you waiting for? I'm sure that Dr. Burke will be able to cover for you for a few more days. When last did you actually have a real holiday Madison?"

"Er, um… I guess when David and I got married?"

"Madison, you do realize that you're talking about five years ago. Not even the main administrator of the hospital is here permanently. Don't you think you at least owe yourself a chance to see whether this relationship could go anywhere?"

"Who said anything about a relationship? You know what my thoughts on relationships are after the fiasco with David."

"Yeah sure, but you're not talking about David here Madison; you're talking about the guy you've been crushing on since you were a geeky teenager in braces. You can't let this opportunity fall through the cracks. If you do, I can see misery in both our futures with way too many tubs of Rocky Road!"

"Look at the time already Lexie. How am I supposed to make any arrangements at this hour? It's too late. I've already told him that I need to get back home. Urgh, why does it have to be Brad Anderson? And why does he need to be so goddamn sexy?"

"Leave it with me. Let me see what I can do from this side. We are still a few hours ahead of you at least." With that, Lexie hung up.

Madison wasn't really holding her breath; she was just incredibly sad that everything had boiled down to a single magical evening spent with the man of her dreams. Except he was no longer the man of her dreams. Feeling incredibly light-headed and drowsy, she managed to doze off dreaming of the tenderness of his goodnight kiss and how his embrace sent shivers throughout her body. There was no denying it, she had fallen for Brad hook, line, and sinker. Right now, she was praying that Lexie could pull off a miracle.

Chapter 9: Napa Valley

Madison was awakened by the concierge calling up to her room.

"Dr. Watson, Mr. Brad Anderson asked me to let you know that he's waiting for you in the Oceanview Café. He said to take your time."

Geez, what time was it? Madison began to panic. She grabbed her phone and was quite relieved to see that it was only 7:00 a.m. No individual in their right mind would expect any woman to be dressed, ready, and packed up by then. She hadn't even undressed from the night before.

Jumping into the shower, Madison knew she would have to move quickly if she was planning on meeting Brad within a reasonable amount of time. She decided to send him a quick text message explaining that he would have to wait a while before she was done. Pressing send, she suddenly felt as though she had butterflies in the pit of her stomach. That definitely wasn't because of the champagne.

Brad sat watching the sunrise over the ocean on a beautiful day. He knew that Madison wouldn't be ready, but couldn't wait a moment longer to see her. Reading her text, he sighed with a broad smile on his face. *Women will be women, they will always keep us waiting.*

Meanwhile back in the suite, Madison was frantically packing, trying to decide what to wear that would be suitable and comfortable for her flight home. She was definitely not going to be caught unaware as she'd been while flying here. She made sure that she was looking decent, if not professional.

Catching a final glimpse at herself in the mirror, apart from her hair that she'd scrunched up in a ponytail, she was satisfied with her appearance.

A bellhop was instantly at the elevator to help her with her bags.

"Where will I find the Oceanview Café?" she asked the bellhop and he guided her to the restaurant.

Upon seeing her again, Brad stood up, once again blown away by how beautiful she was.

"Madison, you're looking especially lovely as always. Are you ready for our trip?" Along with a light pair of chinos, his light blue pinstripe casual shirt and white collar with the top two buttons undone gave her a peek at his chiseled chest. The shirt complimented his eyes as he slowly began undressing her mentally.

"Er... our trip? You mean my trip back to Baltimore. That's where I'm going, isn't it?"

"Not quite. I've managed to arrange for you to take some time off. Dr. Burke will stay on in Baltimore and help out for as long as necessary. I spoke with Colin Jennings, the hospital administrator, last night. He agrees that you deserve some rest and relaxation, especially after the kind of year you've just had.

He was skirting the issue of her divorce and she wasn't quite sure whether it was to protect her or to avoid her from having to relive it.

"So, then where are we going?" It felt like 10,000 butterflies had taken up residence in her stomach.

"It's a surprise!" was all she was going to get from him as he directed her toward the Silver Lexus LC convertible parked directly in front of the hotel.

She'd truly enjoyed her stay at the Hyatt Regency and would be sorry to see the back of the Spanish influenced architecture of the building and the rows of palm trees standing like sentries guarding the hotel pool. It was a glorious day though, and a drive may be just what she needed to try to get all the thoughts running through her head at 500 miles an hour to slow down.

Preparing herself for a comfortable drive, she was shocked as Brad drove through the private entrance to the airport once more. As promised, Edward was waiting at the bottom of the stairs to the Gulfstream.

"Mr. Anderson, Dr. Watson, welcome back. Please allow me to take your luggage."

Brad made way for her to climb the stairs in front of him. Just knowing he was so close made her checks become warm and flushed. He made himself comfortable on one of the longer leather loungers on the plane and motioned for her to sit next to him. Wherever they were going, Madison knew that it was about to get hot and steamy pretty fast. Sitting so close to him, she was able to enjoy the smell of his Clive Christian No. 1 aftershave with its woody undertones. It was going to be challenging on this flight for her to behave, especially after that gentle kiss last night.

"Something to drink?" Edward snapped her back to reality.

"Surprise us," was all that Brad answered.

Given that it was only 9:00 a.m., she was a bit surprised to be drinking so early, but what the heck, she and Lexie had occasionally pulled all-nighters and just carried on drinking in the morning. It was a bit of a regular thing while she was trying to help her get over David.

David? Who the hell cares when you're sitting on a jet with the man of your dreams?

Edward returned with a tray of refreshing Mai Tai cocktails which had been blended to perfection.

The colorful liquid is out of this world. I could quite easily get used to this lifestyle. What are you on about Madison? Are you out of your mind? You know that Brad's just a playboy and you are the flavor of the day. Are you really buying into all of this?

Oh shut up! Can't I just go along with it for a while? I haven't been out with anyone since David. As a matter of fact, I've actually never even known what it's like to have anyone other than David and look at how that turned out. You know this is a bad idea, right? Well, let's give it a couple of days and see what happens.

Once again, she was allowing her thoughts to get the better of her.

Meanwhile, Brad was wondering what she thought of all the attention and luxury. He was really hoping that she wasn't as shallow as most of the other women he's dated, if you could actually call that dating. More like heavy flirting with benefits. Sure, he'd played the field, he'd had countless conquests on his arm, on his jet, and in his bed. This would be the first person he'd ever taken to his Napa Valley property since he acquired it a few short months ago. If it was privacy they were after, they would definitely get it there. Nobody even knew of his latest acquisition, except for Donovan, who had co-signed for the property with him as part of a tax write-off under the business' name.

He was certainly enjoying being so close to Madison, although he was not quite sure of what to make of their relationship just yet. He wanted to explore it further, without having to worry about interruptions and her rushing to get back to Baltimore. What the hell would he do if that was her decision? He had fallen for her like a ton of bricks. There was nobody he'd ever dated or met before that had such an immediate physical effect on him. Given all his dating rules, he was about to throw his own rule book completely out the window.

"We'll be landing within the next 15 minutes, Mr. Anderson."

"Thank you, Edward."

"Landing where?"

"At Oakland International Airport, Dr. Watson. The car will be waiting for Mr. Anderson."

"Uh huh," she replied matter-of-factly.

Brad was looking forward to the 50-mile drive to the villa that he had just bought as part of an investment and a "get away from it all" holiday home. It was actually much bigger than his home in Palo Alto, but the idea was that Brown, Anderson & Associates would entertain at the villa as well from time to time. The last time he was there was before the villa had been redecorated and so Brad was really not sure what he would be walking into.

Taxiing onto the runway at Oakland, Brad once again allowed Madison to walk directly in front of him. There were many little gestures that she was noticing about him, like how he would put his hand gently onto the small of her back, as if it were the most natural thing for him to do. As promised, another town car was waiting directly at the bottom of the jet's stairs. This time, there was more than just Madison's bag and she felt a tinge of excitement in the air. Deciding not to ask where they were going, she was surprised to feel as though she trusted Brad so completely, especially after only one date.

Was it because he had been the gentleman that he was, or was it because she had actually known him during all their time at school? Had he always been this kind to everyone? She really couldn't remember. What she did remember was the nasty little bitch that he used to date—Bethany. Wondering whatever became of her, Madison decided not to ask Brad for fear of letting the cat out of the bag. He very clearly couldn't remember her from Huntington Bay High School, so what would be the use in bursting that bubble right now?

Sitting in the back seat of the town car gave her time to take in the glorious scenery as she realized that they were probably on their way to Napa Valley. Gazing out the window, she was suddenly startled as Brad took her tiny hand into both of his again and pressed them towards his mouth where he delicately planted a kiss on the inside of her palm. She was very grateful that she was sitting down, because her knees would have definitely given way.

What is it about this man that has me so mesmerized and confused at the same time? I can't read him, but there's such softness behind his eyes. They actually look a bit sad and she wasn't prepared to press for further details. There was something that had either happened or that he was thinking about that was too painful for him to think about discussing.

Instead of allowing her hand to return to the seat next to them, he interlocked his long, masculine fingers in between her tiny dainty ones and gazed into her eyes as if trying to communicate something to her.

What Brad was feeling was such a deep longing for the creature next to him, but he was also so afraid of messing things up. The last thing he wanted to do was to chase her away. He'd done as much research on Madison Watson as he felt he could possibly do—with the information that was on the internet. He'd even secretly enlisted the help of her friend, Alexa James (whom he'd never met), to help him arrange for Madison's time off of work. Next to Brad and the villa full of staff, Alexa and the driver were the only people who knew exactly where they were headed.

Madison's heart was pounding in her chest so hard, that she felt it was going to burst. *Just by Brad's simple kiss on the palm of my hand—oh, yes please! Can you kiss me like that all over?* And even with their hands interlocked, her hand felt comfortable and safe with him. She knew that if he could control himself last night with her little burgundy ensemble, he would take things as slow or fast as she wanted. For once in her life, Madison realized that she was totally in control of the relationship and the situation—something she never had with David.

Damn it, why do I keep going back to thinking about David? This is seriously a problem. Am I going to compare him to Brad in every instance? It would be difficult to actually compare David with Brad. Brad has culture, breeding, and manners, and I really believe that he would never do anything to intentionally hurt me. Or at least I would hope not!

Turning off of one of the main roads, they entered a long driveway that had evenly spaced conifers lining the drive on one side. The other side was lined with vineyards, and row upon row of grapevines, laden with fruit as far as the eye could see. Even the drive up to the villa was exquisite. What Madison wasn't ready for, however, was what appeared beyond the conifers as they reached the end of the drive. The villa brick and slate two-story mansion appeared to go on forever. With definite Spanish-style architectural influence, the villa was surrounded by lush greenery and most of the walls were covered with ivy, giving the villa a warm, welcoming feel. The grounds were surrounded by rich, green, rolling lawns cut to perfection and professionally maintained. The roof of the villa was covered with beautiful baked terracotta tiles.

Meeting them at the front door was an entire artillery of staff. Madison's heart sank. She really was looking forward to time alone with Brad to see whether the chemistry they had been feeling since their eyes first met in Baltimore more than 2 months ago was still strong. She was determined to make the most of it, nonetheless.

"So, Mr. Anderson, are you going to do me the honor of showing me around?" Brad felt a little sheepish seeing as he had only been in the villa once before. He had visited several months ago just to look at it before the documents were sent to his office for signing. All communication with the interior designers had been done over the internet via video conferencing. He had an inkling where the bedrooms were and headed in that general direction, following one of the staff who carried their bags.

Under the assumption that Brad and Madison were a couple, the staff members who took their bags took them both through to the main bedroom. They were beginning to unpack when Madison came in behind them.

"No, no, no!" she insisted. "We're not together." We'll be needing two rooms!"

Brad smiled.

"You take the main bedroom and I'll make myself comfortable down the hall."

"Are you certain? I'm also quite fine in any of the other rooms!"

"Not at all. I insist. As a matter of fact, put your swimsuit on and let's go and have lunch down by the pool."

Madison was pleased that she had managed to get a bit of sun on her skin the day before. She could think of nothing worse than being poolside with this Adonis of a man, him all gloriously tanned, and her appearing as a ghost. She imagined that he spent a great deal of time outdoors, especially living it up in luxury, from what she had seen of him so far.

Nothing could be further from the truth. Donovan had threatened to dissolve their partnership if Brad didn't take some time off to relax and rejuvenate. When he heard about Matthew Carmichael, he insisted that Brad fly back to Huntington to be with his old friend. All the while that Brad was away, he'd been constantly stressing about work, calling Donovan every few hours for an update. Donovan had responded simply, reminding Brad to be sure to show Dr. Watson a good time, and to have some time off himself.

Before heading down to the pool, Madison found an oversized white button-up shirt that she could pull over her bikini and the sarong. She was trying to avoid looking naked, especially in front of Brad. Before she knew it, she was being directed down to the terraced section where a long, pale blue swimming pool ran the entire length of the garden complete with lounge chairs on both ends, as well as places for daytime play and evening dining. She was feeling a stirring deep within as Brad suddenly appeared in front of her.

He was wearing plain black swimming trunks with a shirt that was completely open, revealing what she had already suspected, rock hard abs and a six-pack that would make any woman swoon.

Dom Perignon was already on ice in a wine cooler under some hanging patio shade umbrellas. This was placed next to comfortable wicker chairs, as well as freshly squeezed orange juice on ice. There were platters of fresh fruit, cheeses, and finger sandwiches that would have been enough to feed a small army.

"Mimosa?"

"Ooh, yes please! I must admit that I'm suddenly feeling rather parched."

"You must have something to eat as well. The chef doesn't understand how to prepare smaller portions yet. It's going to be a bit of a learning experience for them. They're used to catering much bigger parties. I know that this is probably all overwhelming for you, but I haven't been here to the house since I bought it. I wanted you to be the first to see it!"

There went her entire theory that Brad was nothing but a player who chased women, or at least entertained them by wining and dining them. Seems like he was nothing like that at all. Brad broke her concentration with a Mimosa.

"When you're done, come and join me in the pool, he whispered in her ear." Just his breath that close to her skin brought back memories of his gentle kiss the night before. How she longed for him to take hold of her again, to be back in his arms and to further explore what had surely just been him teasing her to get a reaction.

Removing her sunglasses, shirt and sarong, and kicking off her sandals, she ran and dived into the pool like a schoolgirl on the first day of summer vacation. The water was cool on her skin, yet not icy. It was completely refreshing to be able to swim in peace and freedom without having to worry about other hotel guests ogling from behind tinted sunglasses. In fact, the only person she needed to worry about, she was about to catch up with.

Sensing her behind him, he turned to face her. Suddenly, everything was beginning to become very real for both of them. The sun shone directly behind Brad's head, creating a halo effect and to Madison, he looked like an angel. She dared place one of her hands on his chest close to his heart which seemed to be beating as rapidly as hers. He reached out to pull her closer to him. It was now just the flimsiest of swimsuits between them and possibly several molecules of water.

For the first time, Brad bent down, drawing her up close toward him and devoured her with his mouth. For the first time in her life, Madison knew what it was like to be kissed by somebody who really meant it. She wasn't prepared to stop just yet; her own hunger and desires were coming to the fore and now she knew that he had not been mocking her or playing on her emotions. If this was what his kisses felt like, she didn't want to even think about sleeping with this man.

She was pleased that they were in a pool where she could remain buoyant in his arms, rather than a crumpled mess on the floor, sure that her legs would betray her. She could feel him becoming aroused and this made their passionate embrace even more intense.

"I've been wanting to do that since the very moment I laid eyes on you in Baltimore!"

"I'll bet you use that line often, Mr. Anderson," was all that she could respond, instantly regretting her remarks the moment they escaped her lips.

"Madison, what more do I need to do to prove myself to you? I have never brought anyone here and wouldn't want to be here with anyone other than you. Since Baltimore, you're the only person I can think of. I wake up thinking of you, I fall asleep thinking of you, you're in my dreams, and I honestly don't know what to do about it. I have to know whether you feel the same way about me."

"I think that you can tell by my reaction to your kisses that I do. Thank you for making me take this time off. I would also like to see where this is going to go. But how is this ever going to work between us? You are on the west coast and I am on the east coast. I simply can't give up everything that I've worked for at Johns Hopkins."

"Can we talk about this more?" Let's go and have something to eat and we can see what options we can consider." With that, he scooped her up in his arms, carrying her up the steps to where their towels were draped over two lounge chairs. Once she'd dried herself, she settled back on one of the lounge chairs. Brad found himself next to her, offering to rub suntan lotion on her back. Still fascinated by her tiny frame and flawless complexion, his hands gently worked the lotion all over her. Realizing how much she was turning him on, Brad stopped, grabbing a towel to hide the raw evidence of his lust for this tiny creature.

Leaning toward her, he gently whispered in her ear, "You, Madison Watson, are driving me crazy! I don't know if I can survive another day without you."

Madison looked at him through her ultra-long lashes, with her own deep sense of longing.

Could this finally be Mr. Right? She had always thought so at school. Or was this just a schoolgirl fantasy?

Chapter 10: Always and Forever

Later that afternoon, Brad insisted that they take a drive through the vineyards and to the winery attached to the estate. Madison was feeling so relaxed for the first time in many years, that she would have agreed to almost anything. Realizing that they were traveling in Brad's Lexus LC, she wasn't sure whether or not she needed a scarf for her hair. Deciding to leave it to just blow in the hot Mediterranean heat of Napa Valley, she left it loose.

The trip to the winery was fascinating and they got to taste various wines that were distinct to the vineyards along the estate. The wine that they were most known for was a full-bodied Cabernet Sauvignon. Instructing the winery to have a case delivered to the house, Brad couldn't resist stealing another long, romantic kiss from Madison in the car before heading back to the villa. She'd pulled on a short pair of denim shorts over her swimsuit, along with a tight, white T-shirt with a plunging neckline. Brad's eyes were consuming her unashamedly.

"Don't get changed. I've arranged for us to have some cocktails at the hot tub."

"Hot tub?"

"Yes, there's a rather large one just off the terrace outside your bedroom. It's totally private and secluded. Can we pick up where we left off this afternoon?"

There was nothing more that Madison wanted right then than to give herself totally over to him. At the same time, she was afraid that he would be disappointed in her. She needed to push each of the thoughts away. How would she know if they were compatible and if this relationship had any chance whatsoever unless she was prepared to risk it all?

Throwing caution to the wind, she decided to wear the rather risqué one piece swimsuit instead. Was she trying to get into Brad's head, or his bed? Either way, this would definitely make him go even more gaga over her. Her plan was perfectly executed, as she met him at the hot tub which was accessible through two massive sliding doors from the main bedroom. Leaving the doors open had also been a bit of a strategic move on her part. She wanted to communicate with him psychologically that her bedroom door was wide open.

The message wasn't lost on him either. Still wearing the black swimming trunks, he was already seated in the steamy hot tub with all its jets running. Removing the towel from around her as she stepped closer to the hot tub, all that Brad had to say was, "Madison, why are you doing this to me? If you are playing games with me, then these are very dangerous ones indeed."

"I would never dare play games with you, Bradley Anderson. I am just as serious about seeing where this is going to go as you are!" He was obviously taken by the black swimsuit that she was wearing, and it showed by the increasing bulge in the front of his trunks. He wasn't even trying to hide it from her anymore. In fact, he drew her towards him and gently placed one of her hands on the front of his trunks, whispering in her ear, "Do you notice the effect you're having on me? I simply cannot control myself around you anymore."

Staring up into his blue eyes, for the first time in her life, Madison had never wanted any man more than how she wanted him then. She had been 100% correct when she was that geeky schoolgirl and felt that Bradley Anderson was the only man for her. He had filled her dreams for countless nights while she was at school, and ever since she saw him across the room in Baltimore, she wanted to surrender herself to him completely, but was still wary of every man, thanks to dumbass David.

To say she had trust issues would be a complete understatement. She knew that had Lexie been here, she would be coaxing Madison on to make a complete go of it.

Sensing her reluctance, he allowed her to pull away, not quite sure what to make of what seemed to be a complete 180-degree turn from earlier on. Taking the opportunity to break some of the tension between them, he opened one of the bottles of Cabernet Sauvignon that had been sent from the winery. Pouring two glasses, he offered Madison one of them.

"I'm sorry if I assumed that you feel the same way about me as I'm feeling about you, Madison. Please forgive me if I've offended you. It's the last thing I ever want to do."

"You haven't offended me at all Brad, and you're right. I do feel the same way about you. You're making it extremely difficult to get my thoughts straight. I really want this, but I'm not sure how it's ever going to work with an entire country between us. After my ex, the last thing I need right now is someone playing with my emotions."

"How could you even suspect that? I think you can tell that I'm being serious with you. Madison, I have never had anyone challenge me the way you do. You are unlike anyone else I've ever met before. Apart from being physically attracted to you, I'm in love with your mind! You are intelligent, fiercely independent, and headstrong. I know that you really wouldn't be here unless you wanted to be. I also don't want to hold you here against your will."

Madison could sense a tinge of sadness in his voice. She realized that what she'd said had hurt him, which wasn't her intention at all. Although the sun was beginning to set, she noticed that the sparkle that had been in his eyes seemed to have disappeared. She owed it to him to explain herself.

"Brad, I made a decision when I got divorced that I wouldn't simply fall for the first guy to tip his hat in my direction. That's not necessarily you because I think I know you well enough by now that I know you'd never intentionally hurt me. But we need to be realistic. How do you see this relationship working?"

"I don't have any of the answers for you yet Madison, but all that I know is that I've never felt this way about another living soul! I can't bear the thought of you not being a part of my life. Can't we at least give it a try, rather than ignoring the feelings that we clearly have for one another?"

With that, Brad was next to her once more, pulling her close to him. His lips began gently planting kisses on her moist neck, and moving gently to her ear.

"Oh Madison, you are driving me crazy! How can someone as gorgeous, intelligent, and independent even be here with me?" he whispered in her ear. "Before I get totally carried away, cheers! Thank you for coming with me to the villa for a few days. Here's to whatever the future holds!"

"Cheers!" Madison felt a twinge of regret for having basically shot the man of her dreams down in flames. Would he now send her packing? She didn't have long to wonder. Brad placed his glass down and headed back to where she was seated with the pulsating jets massaging every inch of her body. Placing his hands on her tiny hips, he gently pulled her from the seat of the hot tub until she was standing directly in front of him.

Oh boy, he's definitely not going to stop or give up! Not that I want him to. His touch is so much gentler than David's ever was. I want to tell him to stop, but then again I don't. What's wrong with me? I'm falling totally in love with this man— something that's not hard to imagine, given what I felt about him during high school. I don't want anything to come between us, not even that. Do I dare tell him who I am, or at least, who I was?

By that time, Brad was gently caressing her shoulders and her upper arms. He playfully tugged at the straps on her swimsuit to see whether he's going to get a reaction from her. All that he's getting is an audible moan that's clearly one of pleasure. Behind her, he gradually slipped each strap from the top of her shoulders, kissing each of her arms lightly, all the way down to the palms of her hands. The top of her swimsuit was loose enough to reveal two perfectly perky breasts, where her nipples were standing erect in anticipation.

She leaned back against his chest with her moist raven hair clinging to his wet skin. Groaning, she allowed him to fondle each of her breasts, groaning in anticipation.

"Oh Brad, please stop teasing me. You have no idea what you're doing to me… " Her voice trailed off into another muffled cry.

"Madison, I want you! I need you! But I need you to know that I never sleep with anyone this early in a relationship. Then again, I don't classify you as just anyone!"

"I need you too," she found herself saying, despite her fear that there was no way she would live up to his expectations after all of his other conquests. She'd only ever been with David. What if she disappointed him? She'd wanted to know what he felt like ever since high school. How bad could she really be?

"I never want this day to end!" Not waiting for a second invitation, Brad climbed out the hot tub, held his hand out to Madison, who was fixing her swimsuit, just in case one of the staff happened to be around. She grabbed her towel and headed back to the main bedroom. Brad collected the Cabernet Sauvignon and their glasses, following hot on her heels.

Feeling a bit like that geeky schoolgirl, Madison wasn't sure what to do next. Brad wasn't going to let her skip a beat though and motioned for her to join him in the shower. The on-suite bathroom was huge and consisted of a double shower, a large semi-circular bath, double wash basins, floor to ceiling mirrors, and built-in skylights to add to the overall ambiance.

Brad had climbed into the shower, and just the sight of his muscular, naked body was enough to send Madison into a complete tailspin. *Well, here goes nothing* she thought to herself, removing the swimsuit from her body and stepping in after him. Brad allowed himself to take in everything with his eyes before he pulled her closer in a firm embrace. He insisted on helping Madison wash her back and her hair, and he was completely blown away by her nakedness so close to him.

Unable to contain himself anymore, he had to have her right there in the shower. Gently lifting her up, he held her with both her legs wrapped around his lean, muscular frame. As he penetrated her, Madison gasped, and Brad let out a masculine groan. They began moving together as one, Brad forcing himself deeper and deeper inside her, while Madison could feel herself becoming hotter and wetter as they climaxed together. She was afraid that she'd left scratch marks up and down his back as she worked her way to orgasm. Whimpering, she buried her soaking wet hair and face, into the golden locks of Brad's chest.

He was breathing heavily, and she could feel his heart beating in time with her own as if they were about to beat right out of their chests. *Well, I don't think that either of us let the other one down.*

Finally regaining composure, they climbed out of the shower. Brad insisted on picking her up and carrying her over to the oversized king-size bed.

"Do you mind if I sleep here tonight with you Madison? I just can't let you out of my sight. I know that if I do, I might wake up to find that I'm dreaming." All that she could manage was a nod. She was still trying to get her hormones into check following the encounter in the shower.

Brad had simply wrapped a towel around his torso, and she was admiring how fit and lean he was. It had been more than a year since she'd last had sex. Not that she could call tonight sex. Whatever she had with David was just plain sex. What she'd experienced with Brad this evening was pure ecstasy.

The remainder of the evening was spent making love, exploring one another's bodies, and finding sensitive spots. Madison lost count of the number of times Brad was able to get her to climax, each time being gentle with her. She had no idea what time they eventually fell asleep, and neither did she care to know. All she cared about was being safe and securely nestled in his arms.

***

Time seemed to stand still while she was at the villa and Madison was dreading having to leave to return to Baltimore. She knew that they had touched on the subject just after she'd arrived, but so much had happened since then. All that she knew was that she was well and truly in love with Brad

Anderson. She finally understood where the lean, athletic build came from. He was extremely disciplined in his daily exercise routine—something she never really worried about because she was constantly running up and down within the hospital.

During the day, he would take her to interesting places in Napa Valley. They'd spent time at the pool, in the hot tub, or making wild, passionate love. Evenings were filled with fine dining experiences, followed by making love into the early hours of the morning. Brad had been the first to tell Madison that he loved her.

She was quite taken aback, when he expressed how he felt about her, and she knew that she felt exactly the same way. Hell, she'd been in love with him ever since high school. How does she tell him that, without him thinking that she was a complete fraud, or realizing what a geek she was and changing his mind about how he felt about her? She knew that if they were to have any kind of future at all though, she would have to tell him at some stage. When would be the right time though? The longer they were together, the more of a fraud Madison was feeling like.

"Lexie, I need your advice and I need you to think quickly and on your feet."

"Hey, you! Don't I always think on my feet? I'm the sharpest pencil out there!" Lexie laughed. She had still not told Madison of her involvement in arranging her leave with Brad.

"Brad has told me he loves me now on a number of occasions. You know how I feel about him, and that I've been in love with him forever. I need to tell him who I really am Lexie, and I don't know how."

"Well, Madison, there are only a couple of options that I can see from my point of view. You need to be straight-up honest with him. If you can't do it face-to-face, then I suggest you write him a letter explaining yourself. Don't worry about it my friend, it will all work out just the way it should in the end!"

Hanging up with Lexie, she knew what she needed to do. She needed to get back to Baltimore as soon as possible, and escape this situation. She was only making it worse for herself to have to admit everything to Brad. She'd sit down and write him a letter explaining everything; all about who she was, her schoolgirl crush that she'd had on him, how she hadn't been completely upfront and honest with him when he'd asked about her past, and all of it. She'd also own up to the fact that she'd never felt this way about anyone in her life, but that their relationship simply could never be a reality. The distance was too great and before things became even more entangled, it was best for her to walk away now.

Knowing that Brad had a very high standard of ethics and honesty, she was sure that her letter would be accepted by him as being a sign from the universe that they were never meant to be.

One last night of being in his arms and she'd have to settle with the knowledge that she could have possibly had it all. Madison was tired of pretending and felt that Brad deserved to know the truth.

While he was out for his morning run, Madison was climbing into an Uber and heading toward the Oakland International Airport. She'd booked herself onto a single flight, traveling home to Baltimore. Unable to hide her emotions any longer, she used her Ray Bans to cover her emerald green eyes that were filled with tears.

The seven or so hours of flying coach should help her try and figure out what she was going to do with the rest of her life, having just walked away from the best thing to ever happen to her.

Boarding the Southwest flight, she had only brought a smallish purse and her tablet with her as well as her travel pillow. The rest of her luggage was checked. Finding her seat and settling in, she began wondering whether she'd made the right decision telling Brad. It was too late now for any regrets and she just hoped that he was willing to forgive her.

Several hours later, the airline attendants notified all passengers to fasten their seatbelts as they were coming in to land at Washington D.C. International Airport. Feeling the rush of adrenaline as the massive Airbus touched down safely with the wing flaps creating resistance to bring the plane to a standstill, Madison breathed a sigh of relief. She was only too grateful to have arrived in Baltimore in one piece. Now to grab her luggage and hail a cab to drop her off at her apartment.

Waiting at the conveyor belt for her luggage, she was hardly aware of the tall figure approaching her from behind. She was still wearing her Ray Bans and was sure her eyes would give her away to anyone who even remotely looked happy or in love. Before she could reach for her bags, they were being whisked off the conveyor belt and placed on a luggage trolley. Turning around, Madison recognized Steve. She could have hugged him right then and there for being a familiar face.

It was only after that, that she saw Brad standing with a massive bouquet of red roses. Madison could no longer hold back her tears. Running toward him, she gave him one of the biggest hugs ever.

"Madison, I always knew who you were!"

“Wha... what? You knew it was me all along, but you never said anything?”

“Well, put it this way, I knew who you were from the time I asked for you to come to Huntington to see what you could do for Matthew. It has never mattered to me who you were, or whether you wore braces or not. The only thing that matters to me is you. I want to spend the rest of my life with you Maddie Watson! Will you marry me?”

Brad had gone down on one knee in front of the entire airport and opened a box with an exquisite champagne diamond in a classic setting, with delicate vintage swirls on either side of the four claws. “I’m not standing up until you say yes!”

“Of course I’ll marry you Brad. I have and will love you always and forever!”

www.ingramcontent.com/pod-product-compliance
Lightning Source LLC
Chambersburg PA
CBHW071919120726
48001CB00005B/1789